Starving Writers
Literary Journal

Volume 2

"The Love of Literature"

February 2019

Starving Writers Literary Journal- Volume 2

February 2019

A Truesource Publishing Book

Truesource Publishing : Dallas Texas

www.truesourcepublishing.com

ISBN : 978-1-932996-69-2

Printed in the United States of America
Published in Dallas, Texas

Editors
Marcus Blake
Jenn Chastka
Camila Gonzalez
Andrew Fallman

For More information on Starving Writers...

www.starvingwriters.net
www.facebook.com/starvingwritersjournal
www.twitter.com/starvingwritersjournal

"Start writing, no matter what. The water does not flow until the faucet is turned on."

~ Louis L'Amour

Table of Contents

©2014 Debbie Ridpath Ohi. URL: Inkygirl.com. Twitter: @inkyelbows.

Check out more cartoons like this….
www.inkygirl.com

SHORT STORIES

MALBIHN

By

J. Franklin Green

Avarice and adventurers are dangerous companions. Hired to seek out a fortune and a myth, a rough-cut, unsavory man finds more than he bargains for in the Arizona wilderness.

BIG KARL

"Karl, that was an incredible trip. It was worth the wait and every penny we paid. Millions of people do Grand Canyon river expeditions, helicopter fly overs, Phantom Ranch hikes and even the Supai Falls and Havasupai Reservation Village but your guided trip down from Utah through the upper reaches was just, - well, priceless is the only word." The well- tanned, weather-beaten man reached into his pack and pulled out his wallet. "Here's and extra five hundred for you. All six of us pitched in."

Bill Harder reached out his hand, but 'Big Karl Malbihn' gave it a perfunctory shake, stuffed the money in his sweat stained shirt pocket and muttered a barely audible "thanks."

The rest of the group was already getting into the van that would bring them to the Hualapai Reservation Lodge where comfortable, albeit expensive rooms were waiting as well as their private vehicles that had been driven down from Utah by young reservation Indians hired for that purpose. Malbihn paid the boys crap wages, but they liked driving the Land Rovers, BMWs, Mercedes and other high end cars that they would never own for the 15 hour drive down to Arizona.

Karl was not sorry to see the group leave. They had been competent enough hikers, except for Harder, and of course, had all the best high-end equipment their rich asses could buy. But two weeks of listening to them and their snooty, chitchat around the campfire was more than enough for him. Mergers, acquisitions, private jet flights all over the world and their fancy homes held little interest to him and in fact, rather pissed him off. He would never have that kind of money. Not that he wouldn't want to. *'Two weeks of guiding these rich suckers, cooking for them, patching up their minor injuries and toting half of Harder's gear half the frigging   time, and all they could scrape up was a lousy extra five hundred,"* he thought sourly. *"They probably drop that on a fancy dinner in some resort or Manhattan restaurant."*

Malbihn himself had never eaten in a New York City high- end restaurant, or any other kind, because he had never been east of the Mississippi. He had been born in Wisconsin to a poor family and dropped out of high school after the eleventh grade. After ten years of odd jobs in stores, ranches, and farms, he got a job with his old pal Sven Jenssen up in Canada doing wilderness camping tours. Whatever a perverse benevolent nature had lacked, giving him between the ears, it made up for with his rugged physique and crude but practical mind. It had also bequeathed him a violent temper, and gruff personality, which he honed and developed over his nearly forty-five years. Few men messed with him and few women could put up with him. Blonde haired, with icy blue eyes, he stood well over six foot four with broad shoulders and the muscles of a professional athlete. Tiring of the bitter cold winters of the north, he migrated to Northern Arizona five years ago and started his own private tour company with a small amount of money he inherited from his mother's life insurance. It helped grease a few palms for permits and run a few ads online or in wilderness travel magazines. He also scrounged a few books on Grand Canyon lore, Indians, southwest history and such, so he could talk the talk as well as hike the hike.

The highlands of northern Arizona were windy and chilly in the winter and scorching hot, dry and sun baked in the summer, but far preferable in his mind to the testicle freezing long winters and humid mosquito infested summers of Wisconsin and southern Canada. Six months before starting his business, Malbihn camped out all over the state looking for a unique sales angle and becoming intimately familiar with the environment. He also familiarized himself well with the conservationist mindset of his potential customers.

Turning his back on the group, he stowed his gear, climbed into his well-worn Jeep Wrangler and left them to their comforts. He headed down Indian Route 6 to Peach Springs, a small town on old historic Route 66 where he lived in a dilapidated fifth wheel camper that he rented from an old geezer who had 120 acres littered with shacks, beat-up campers and the usual assortment of trash, litter and junked vehicles. The place also had the usual assortment of critters, coyotes, javelinas, and pack rats. *'Home not-so-sweet home, but at least the rent is cheap'*, he thought as he popped the clutch and spit dust in his wake.

"Same old crap, different bunch of crap heads and same crap pay," he said aloud as he turned off the dirt road onto the paved highway. "Maybe I'll grab a steak at the tavern in town. Beats the hell out of whatever canned food I have at home, and I can use the massive tip they gave me to eat good and maybe find a little female comfort at Muriel's place." He had a week before the next tour. Malbihn never made that trip and the new group never got a refund on their advance payment.

THE PROPOSITION

Malbihn was half way through his 'still movin' rare t-bone and all of the way through three cold beers with a Jim Beam chaser, when an immaculately dressed man carrying a cane slipped into the booth across from him in Ralph's Route 66

Tavern. His clothes were straight out an L.L. Bean catalog with a short shot of REI or Cabella's tossed in. The cane had an intricately carved brass handle that screwed into the top. As a contrast to Malbihn's sweat stained shirt, vest and thick blonde beard, he was smooth shaven and wore thin wire rimmed glasses.

"Who the hell are you, and what do you want?" Malbihn said gruffly with half a chewed mouthful, some of which exited in the general direction of the intruder on his supper.

"My name is J. Morrison Baynes, III," the man said softly. Before your well-known reputation for mayhem, maladjusted moody disposition, or malodorous personality kicks in, let me first say, that the dinner and drinks are on me. It is already paid for in full, with a handsome tip for Susie over there at the bar."

Malbihn glanced in her direction, and she flashed him a big smile and a thumbs up. He decided to hold back with the epithet he was about to unleash, and cut another chunk of steak.

"In addition to that, there is a very nice looking young Asian lady waiting for you at Muriel's, how would you say it, palace of female delight. Also paid in advance. Said young woman will have no other companions than you for the next two days. Muriel herself will make sure of that, and it was in fact, she whom advised me that I would likely find you here today."

Baynes paused for a moment to let this sink in. Malbihn cut another large piece of beef, forked it into his mouth and just nodded as if to say, "Go on, you have my attention."

The man slid a small but thick manila envelope across the table just short of Malbihn's plate. "In this envelope is ten thousand dollars in cash and a postdated check for $100,000 more, one year from now, made out to you and only good at the Chase Bank branch on the corner of Thunderbird and Scottsdale Road in Phoenix. I hope that this, in addition to the advance tip, has garnered your attention?" He noted as Malbihn reached for the envelope, a small tattoo on his wrist. It was a small outline silhouette in the shape of Wisconsin and the letters KM/FU beneath. It didn't take a cryptology expert to figure out it was Malbihn's parting sentiment about his home state.

He was interrupted briefly in his speech when Susie brought another beer, a shot glass of bourbon for

Malbihn, and a vodka tonic for Baynes. She was handed a twenty-dollar bill for her efforts, and almost fell out her short skirt as she wriggled away.

Malbihn tossed down the shot followed by a gulp of beer, burped, squinted at Baynes and said, "Who the hell do you want me to kill? As much as I like the money, that's not my gig. I can't spend any damn money from a prison cell."

Baynes replied, "Relax, my burly friend, I have had men killed for far less money. I'm in need of your particular talents and acumen for a far more lucrative venture. For you *and* me."

Malbihn deliberately took the last bite of his steak followed by an equally slow sip of beer. "Okay, boss man, you have my undivided attention." His normal avarice aside, Malbihn reckoned that if this was for real, he could stop earning his living from the sweat running down the small of his back and aching feet. He wasn't getting any younger, and with that amount of dough, he could set up a little outfitters store and hire the Indians to do the guide work.

"You are intimately familiar with this area all the way up into Utah if I am accurately informed," continued Baynes. "I also understand that you are self-reliant and need no retinue of helpers. The expedition I have in mind is strictly a one person operation. And, that one person will need to keep the purpose close to the vest, if you understand my meaning. Very close to the vest. Other than your penchant for the women of the evening and an occasional drink or two or ten, I have it on good reference that you know how to keep important things to yourself."

"Correct on all three of those things," Malbihn replied with a grin, "Although I don't know if I'd use them fancy terms myself."

Baynes returned the grin and continued, "This project may take a while and be extremely difficult, but I believe the incentive I have offered is sufficient. Are you willing?"

"My daddy always told me not to jump in the water until I knew how deep it was, although I have been known to not exactly do that all the time. How deep's the water, and when do I jump?" Malbihn sat back in the booth still chewing the meat and took one more sip.

"Mr. Malbihn, or might I call you, Karl, have you ever heard of *Kwi-ka- kikinee*?"

Malbihn sat forward and laughed hard, spewing no small amount of beer and mouth debris as he did so. "Good God, if there is one. Are you nuts, or do you think I am a total moron? Of course I have, just like everyone else who has been around in the bush, barrooms and boondocks. There ain't no such thing or critter. It's a myth no different than countless others like Bigfoot, or Sasquatch or dozens of other names that myths, mysteries and wild imaginations can conjure up. Come to think of it, maybe I ain't the moron sitting here in this dive."

Baynes sat impassively during Malbihn's tirade, but reached into his vest pocket for yet another envelope that he slid across the table when the laughter stopped. "Please open this and observe. If you are still skeptical afterward, just give it back along with the other envelope, but feel free to partake of my previous offered gifts. We can then part ways and I will continue my search for another such as you. No harm, no foul, as you might say."

Malbihn opened the envelope, which contained three, 5x 7 inch black and white photos. Two were very clear and well lit, but the third had some blurring to it as if the subject or camera had moved slightly. He recognized the background terrain instantly. It was up on the Shivwits Plateau near the Grand Wash Cliff Wilderness Area. The man-like creature depicted was wild looking with hair flowing down well past its shoulders, retained around its head only by a single unadorned rawhide thong. Bushy eyebrows nearly obscuring savage looking eyes were nearly joined by a massive beard, running well up the cheeks and falling down nearly to its waist. The sole garment in evidence was a ragged canvass- like material that ran off one large, muscular shoulder, downward to its hips and wrapped haphazardly about the groin. It was crouched only slightly with open, grasping hands. Two small details attracted Malbihn's attention with no small amount of wonder. Tucked into the garment was what appeared to be a small piece of paper, and in one photo, there was a large gray wolf poised next to him, its shaggy side nearly brushing the creature's left leg.

Malbihn had seen plenty of these types of photos in his time in magazines, curio shops, postcards, and on television. All were grainy or indistinct and could have been shadows or something made out of sticks and rags. Some were so badly retouched that only the most gullible would give them a second l o o k . Although c e r t a i n l y no photography expert, these looked to be very real and the fact that he knew the location from experience added greatly to their believability.

"Do you want me to kill it, capture it or take more pictures of it fellow?"

"As you can see, I have photos already. They cost me a small fortune as it was. The man I hired handed me his Nikon camera just before expiring. The poor soul. Killing it would not yield any profit to me either. Your task, if you think you are up to it, is to capture this Kwi-ka-kikanee and bring him, or it, to me. If you fail, or fail to return, I suppose my search for one capable of the task will perforce continue."

His ego and greed thoroughly aroused, Malbihn replied firmly, "I'm your man. There ain't nothing I know better than Northern Arizona and Southern Utah and I don't need any nursemaids or camp followers neither. But if this is a hoax, or I search for a year and can't find it - I keep the ten grand right?"

"Absolutely my friend, but I suspect you will either become a very rich man, or possibly a corpse. There is an associate of mine here in town whom I trust in any event, has been, like yourself, well paid. He will contact me the moment you report to him or your dead body shows up." Baynes handed Malbihn a business card. "I sincerely hope the former is the result and since you have much to prepare for your endeavor, after, of course, the joys of this evening, I will bid you good day." Baynes arose and left the tavern without looking back other than to tip his hat to the waitress and the bartender.

PREPERATIONS

First light filtered through the lace curtains of a second floor room at Muriel's "boarding house" out on Old Miller road. Chin-Chin, a petite Chinese/Malaysian prostitute lay still sleeping next to Malbihn but he was already fully awake, his mind filled with plans and possibilities. The previous night a day ago was something of a blur. Bourbon and the two girls supplied by the more than willing Muriel occupied his sole attention. Pilar Sanchez had to beg off a second night because she was so sore down below she could barely walk in the morning. Chin-Chin was more than happy to get Pilar's share for a second night. Fortunately for her, Malbihn's appetite had been sated the night before. Muriel herself came in around eleven and gave him a rubdown and back massage, a courtesy that was unheard of, but bespoke more of the hefty financial bonus from Baynes than any affection for her semi-regular and sometimes quarrelsome customer.

As Malbihn gathered his clothing from all points of the room, Chin-Chin watched him from one half-open eye, hoping he would leave, thinking her still asleep. Had this been a normal romp, he would not have hesitated to roughen her awake for a morning quickie, but today he had other things to do. Money trumped women easily in his way of thinking because if you had the former, the women were easy.

Before noon, Malbihn had returned to his place, gathered all his wilderness survival equipment which included a Smith and Wesson .357 revolver, and a fully choked 22 inch 12 gauge shotgun with a wide leather sling, and was heading west on Route 66. He knew his starting point from the photographs. The place was high up in the remote area of the Parashant National Monument well above the Grand Canyon between the border of Arizona and Utah. Not many people in that area if you discounted the fundamentalist Mormons in Colorado City, but they mostly kept close to their homes with their multiple wives and cult religion to avoid unnecessary run-ins with the Arizona State Police. Other than that, there were only a few scattered one-horse towns like Wolf Hole or Tuwleep, infrequent wilderness hikers, hermits and nut balls. The revolver would take care of any trouble with them. His main concern and reason to hurry was a meeting with yet another Sanchez. It was already late May, and old "Turtle Chops Sanchez," a half-breed Hopi Indian, would be closing up shop and moving his herd of horses and burros north for the summer. Unfortunately, there was no direct route. He would have to head west to skirt the Colorado River near Las Vegas, and then turn north, northeast on Interstate 15 up into Utah to get to that old thief's ranch near St. George.

Sanchez was indeed getting ready for the move north to a dude ranch in Wyoming when Malbihn pulled up in front of his dilapidated unpainted three-room shack. A rough corral held in a group of dusty, sad eyed burros. Behind what Sanchez grandiosely called his ranch house, stood a grayish brown barn with missing or rotted boards and an incongruous freshly painted bright green feed shed. Milling around in a corral in front of it was a small herd of eight scrawny, raw boned horses in varying shades of brown, that would soon be the delight of tourists taking selfies and digital group photos imagining themselves to be real wild west cowboys, cowgirls or desperadoes. Two long and rusting horse trailers were standing to one side, only awaiting equally rusting old pickup trucks to hitch up and haul them. Sanchez was standing beside one checking the tires.

Malbihn could care less about the ponies. It was the burros he was really interested in. When it comes down to it, horses are delicate and thirsty critters. A loose shoe, a sharp rock or a twist of an ankle makes them useless in a hurry. Horses also consumed an average of twenty-five gallons of water a day even if not working and a lot of forage and feed. And even broken down trail horses like those who would more or less tolerate a broad tourist dude ranch butt or small child on a tame, nose to tail trail ride will spook easily if out of their normal routine. Burros on the other hand, are tractable, sturdy, steady and used to carrying heavy loads for long periods. They were less needy of water and ate damn near anything they could get their teeth on. A stale muddy pool of water and patches of dried grass or weeds may not be their favorites, but they could survive on them. Knowing what he really wanted, Malbihn of course, started to bargain for the horses. He already had a small stock trailer parked a few miles back on a side road.

"Hey, Turtle Chops my old friend, long time, no see. How's business up this way?" Malbihn knew the answer before he asked. "I'm thinking of doing a little side business down in Peach Springs doing trail rides for the Route 66 tourists. You interested in selling any of your ponies?"

Sanchez eyed him icily. They were certainly not old friends. Malbihn had tried to swindle him several times in the past, but that he didn't really hold against him. Honor among thieves, he expected it, and would have been the swindler himself if he could, but he just wasn't as good at it. He really hated Karl Malbihn for the time he tried to come on to his only granddaughter, but when her boyfriend showed up and objected, Malbihn was in the process of mercilessly beating him senseless, until Sanchez himself showed up with his double barreled shotgun. Malbihn tried to claim self-defense from a jealous lover, but Sanchez knew better. It didn't stop him from doing business with him from time to time however. Money was money after all.

"My friends call me Sanchez," he replied. My ponies ain't for sale unless you can give me a fairer price than you give me for my Ford F150 a year ago."

Malbihn smiled to himself and knew he had a deal going. He started by offering Sanchez a price of about two-thirds of what they were worth for four of the horses. Sanchez just rolled his eyes and spat tobacco juice in the dust. As they haggled, Malbihn inched the price up bit by bit knowing full well what old Turtle Chops could make on them by running trail rides up in Wyoming near Jackson Hole where wealthy summer tourists didn't give two spits what they paid. Sanchez didn't budge, but enjoyed annoying Malbihn.

"Okay Sanchez, you win, I guess I'll have to get some ponies elsewhere. What about the burros? Well-heeled summer dudes ain't gonna want anything to do with them unless it's for a petting zoo for the kiddies. And all the while you'll have to feed 'em and haul all of them up there, or hire someone here to tend them."

Sanchez eyes brightened almost imperceptibly. When the bargaining was done, Malbihn allowed himself to "lose" and paid about twenty percent more than they were worth. Both men were happy. Sanchez got to beat Malbihn and in turn, since Karl had no time to loose, and plenty of chump change in his pocket, he was more than happy to get the three burros he needed. An hour later, he returned with the trailer in tow and managed to get Sanchez to throw in a bale of hay and four old water buckets along with the burro's rope harnesses, beat up old blankets and wooden pack cradles for only fifty bucks more. Just to show there were no hard feelings Malbihn tossed the old man a pouch of Indian Red chewing tobacco as a gift toward future dealings as he drove away. He still had many miles ahead of him before he got to his chosen jumping off point.

AND FOUR TO GO

Karl Malbihn, the three sad eyed burros, and what he hoped would be more than adequate provisions, reached the starting point he selected after a ten-hour drive along a narrow, rock-strewn dirt road near Mount Poverty. Considering his pay and mission, the irony in the name was not lost on him. The last fifteen miles resembled a game trail or cow path. He already had to change two tires, and when the axle of the trailer gave out with a grinding snap, he quit. The burros were unloaded, loaded up with all his gear and they set out. Late May and June could already be scorching hot in southern Arizona, but here in the uplands the nights were still chilly and daytime temperatures ranged from sixty to eighty degrees. Optimistically, he hoped to find his quarry before the deadly heat of high summer, but if he didn't, he was prepared for that too. If need be, he and the burros would lay-up in the heat of the day and travel from dusk to dawn guided by the stars, compass and the usually bright moon.

His immediate goal was the location he recognized from Bayne's photos. Since he adjudged them as recent, he felt sure he could find some sign or spoor. The creature was obviously human and its droppings, tracks and other signs would be easily differentiated from all of the various animals he was already familiar with. Besides, humans usually have at least temporary shelters unlike most wild beasts even if it was only a shallow cave at the bottom of a wash or an arroyo.

"This should be a cake walk," he thought as he was *beginning the steep descent to a shallow valley. This so called Kwi-ka-kikinee, is still just a friggin' myth. That thing in the photo is probably some half-baked, half nuts, wannabe wild man. The wolf threw me off for a minute, but it's probably some cub he took in and raised it from wild. The real tip off was the paper or envelope stuck in his clothes. Probably a photo of some gal that threw him over and made him crazy. Half-naked as he was, he also stays near where that photo was taken. But myth-man or wild man, I'll find him and get paid or I ain't Big Karl Malbihn."*

It took a little over a week of grueling travel to reach the foot of the hills he recognized from the photo. He hadn't actually been this close before, but had seen them from a distance with his high-powered Bushnell binoculars. The ground was rougher and drier than it looked. Stunted wind bent junipers, scraggly chaparral, prickly pear cactus, half-dead cholla and an occasional patch of dry grass that gathered around deep washes was about all the vegetation to be seen. Animal life was more scarce, unless you counted scorpions, striped lizards, the occasional pack rat den and the inevitable rattlesnakes.

"This moron couldn't have picked a more god-forsaken spot to live," he the thought. *"If you want to get away from it all, there's more hospitable places."*

***

As Malbihn crossed a rocky flat, he smelled it before he saw it. The smoke was just a wisp, but the breeze carried the unmistakable odor of burning juniper. It was what he had been expecting for several days. Tethering the lead burro to a stump, he loosened his revolver in it's holster and pulled the shotgun from it's scabbard. Approaching the edge of the deep arroyo quietly, he covered the last few yards on his hands and knees and peered over. What he saw was more or less, what he was expecting. A faded and torn blanket was covering a slight indentation in the south side of the cliff side. The corners were attached to two gnarled poles offering some shade in addition to the north facing where the sun would normally only hit in high summer. The indent wasn't even deep enough to rightly be termed a cave and outside there was a small leather bed and a few other odds and ends he couldn't quite make out. He waited patiently for a quarter hour to survey the entire area and hopefully catch a glimpse of his quarry or possibly his wild wolf companion. Suddenly he felt a burning pain in his left leg, but made no outcry. He didn't even bother to kill the small scorpion as it skittered away, so intent was he on stealth. Besides, he had been stung countless times before. No big deal, really no worse than a wasp or yellow jacket sting and unlike those pests, a scorpion usually only pops you once unless it's caught inside your clothes. He remembered laughing when he saw an old James Bond movie where a scorpion was dropped down one of the bad guy's shirt and he died almost instantly.

"Damn, this was too easy," he thought. *"The ten grand was fine, but to wait for a whole year for the rest? Hell, Baynes should give it to me the minute I get back plus a bonus for speed."* While this was passing through his mind, his eyes were picking out a concealed approach down into the small canyon. Surprise is always best. Chasing down this wild - man was not part of the game plan.

Picking his was down as stealthily as possible, Malbihn approached along the base of the arroyo with shotgun at the ready. As he clicked off the safety, wary of any wolf, he was caught completely off guard by what he heard next.

"I smelled you and your burros a long time ago *white man.* Heard you the minute you started down the arroyo. What took you so long, and what do you want of Go-Yat-Pei?"

Cautiously stepping in front of the blanket lean-to, he saw a withered old Indian, probably Hopi or Navajo, sitting cross- legged cooking what looked mightily like a large lizard over a meager fire. Thoughts of no instant riches combined with the scorpion sting, put Malbihn in an uglier mood than normal.

"You Hopi or Navajo old man? And what the hell are you doing way out here?" Malbihn grumbled. "I haven't seen any tracks or sign for days, which way did you come from, or did you friggin' fly here?"

"I am Apache *white man.* Came up here from the White Mountains of the Mogollan rim country. I tired of watching my people and family turn into fat slaves to the casinos, the welfare of the tribal handouts and white man gifts and greed. I came here to die, but have lived here longer than I thought I would. It has been hard, but I have managed. Hardship and solitude can bring peace to the heart and gifts to the mind. Why are *you* here, *white man*? There is nothing in this land to profit you."

Already aggravated, the old man's continued and purposeful use and emphasis of 'white man' pushed him over to ugly, but he held his temper at bay, in case the old fart might be useful. He leaned the shotgun on a rock and pulled the envelope of photos from his travel pouch. Taking one from the envelope, he slowly approached and handed it to the ancient Apache.

"Have you seen this old man?" Malbihn paused to try to read the old man's expression. "I am looking for him, or it."

Pulling the photo close to his face, the old man squinted to see it better, but his expression remained blank for a moment. Then he smiled, revealing nearly toothless gums, and looked Malbihn squarely in the eye for a full minute.

Bowing his head, he dropped the photo in the sand and said, "*Kwi-ka-kikinee*." Looking up, he continued, "I have seen *Kwi-ka-kikinee* twice in my long lifetime, *white man*. Once when still a teen in the Sitgreaves Forest far southeast of here, and once only, but two to three months ago here in these wastelands." His deeply wrinkled face turned stern and he sat up straighter. "*Kwi-ka-kikinee* is not for one such as you to seek or find. He is immortal, and comes and goes where and when he pleases and with those, he chooses to travel with. Beasts understand him more deeply than any human could. Lucky is the man who sees him and lives. I have been lucky twice. Go home *white man* to your civilized comforts, and your total lack of respect for things you cannot understand and never care to. Leave me to my mission in peace."

Malbihn's face grew dark as he picked up the photo from the ground and stepped back. Turning as though to leave he drew his revolver and turned back toward Go-Yat-Pei. The old Indian showed no sign of surprise or fear, and continued to sit impassively even as Malbihn pulled the trigger. The echo of the gunshot rang down the arroyo like the cry of a wolf.

"Your mission is accomplished you old bastard," Malbihn muttered under his breath.

***

He camped that night in the cover of the arroyo, making use of the old man's fire pit, if not his intended meal. *"The crazy old coot might have had to resort to fillet of roast reptile, but I ain't so incli ned,"* he thought sourly. *"Ain't never gonna be that desperate."* After his supper of beans and dried beef, he tended to the burros who had been unnerved by the gunshot, did a quick rattlesnake check and slid into his sleeping bag.

Sleep normally came easily to him, as it often time does with people of little conscience, but not this night. The good news that he pondered was that the old Indian confirmed that he had seen the creature in the photo. His lecture left little doubt about that. Malbihn swore to himself that he would find and capture it. If the old guy saw it as a young man down in the White Mountains that must have been at least forty to sixty years ago depending on how old the geezer was. Since that time, that whole area had been populated by city folks coming mostly out of Phoenix and putting up swanky cabins. They were really houses, nicer by far than the beat up house he grew up in. Towns and business grew accordingly to accommodate them and the inevitable tourists. He would have set up shop somewhere between Payson and Alpine but couldn't afford the damn rent. He knew a few people who worked in the restaurants and stores there and *they* couldn't afford to live in town! Them, the teachers, cops, firefighters and other public employees were forced to live in the outlying areas. However, that meant that his quarry probably never went down that way anymore or it would have been seen and photographed countless times. That narrowed down the area, he would have to search.

The other thing that kept him awake was killing the old Indian. Shooting the guy didn't bother him, but possibly getting caught did. *"I had to go and lose my temper huh? But the shithead really pissed me off,"* he thought. As remote as the area was, there was always the chance some pain in the ass hiker, naturalist or other jerk would find the body. Then helicopters would come with rangers or cops, investigations made, and it would be possible that he could be implicated. Digging a grave deep enough to be unnoticed would take half a day of hump busting work in the hard and rocky ground. Malbihn had neither the patience nor the tools for the task. Besides, he would also have to erase and traces of the old man's campsite. Still pondering what to do he finally drifted off to sleep to the sound of the wind that mingled almost completely with the distant howl of wolves.

With the coming of dawn came a solution to his dilemma. Fortunately, he had shot the Indian smack dab in the forehead. Women he had been told once by a deputy sheriff usually committed suicide with a gun by shooting themselves in the chest, not wanting to mess up their faces. Men, on the other hand went for the sure thing "bullet straight to the old brain box." Malbihn wiped the gun and unspent cartridges clean and placed it in the dead man's hand. The revolver was unregistered, as are almost all guns in Arizona, and he had gotten it in trade anyway for a poker game debt from some dude he barely knew. The cardboard box of ammo he took from his pack and tossed into the back of the rocky niche along with the old man's other meager possessions. In a couple of days, the weather and scavengers would strip the corpse sufficiently so the fact that there was no powder residue on his head or hand wouldn't be noticed - or probably even looked for. Who the hell, would go to the trouble for an old Indian anyway?

Malbihn only had one regret. He liked the gun. Now he had only his shotgun and two boxes of shells, one for light game and one with heavy deer and predator loads. No more killing people he swore, no matter how much they ask for it.

***

As he was doing this, J. Morrison Baynes was sitting down to lunch at the Boulders Resort in Phoenix, more troubled by fudging his scorecard on the golf links than Malbihn was by killing a man. Later that day, he sought out his golfing companion and returned the hundred-dollar wager on the match.

BUT IT'S A DRY HEAT

June gave-way grudgingly to July and then August and Malbihn was no closer to his often dreamed of hundred grand. The nine thousand four hundred and sixty three dollars he had stashed in his pack was meaningless. Where he was, it couldn't buy him a glass of cold water or a peanut butter and jelly sandwich on stale Wonder Bread. He understood Arizona heat well and had prepared accordingly, but his excursions with the rich tourists rarely lasted more than three weeks. He had been on the trail now for three months. His path described a ragged horseshoe southward to the mountains of the Sanup Plateau near the southernmost bend of the Colorado River. He considered crossing and exploring the Music Mountains area, but discarded the idea as being too hot. Instead, he turned northeast to the Uinkaret.

The hot wind and scorching heat was not taking as much a toll on his body as it was on his mind. As scornful as he was about the tour groups, they at least kept you busy and as irritating as the usually boring conversation was, it was at least some conversation. The two remaining burros didn't complain even though they now had heavier loads. One had tripped over the edge of a deep wash and broken a leg. "Screw you, you clumsy beast," he yelled at the time. "I ain't even gonna waste a shotgun shell on you." The burros said nothing. No request for mercy. No reproach. They just stood wearily and bent to their new task with what remaining strength they had in their rapidly weakening and emaciated frames.

Malbihn now took to making his thoughts verbal. He was driven by three overpowering obsessions. The money, the fame (along with the additional money it would bring), and pride. As time wore on, they intermingled so tightly it was hard for him to separate them.

"Nobody gets the best of 'Big Karl Malbihn,' I've earned every penny of that hundred grand already you shit-for-brains Baynes. That wild sucker really exists, and I'll find him or my name ain't Karl Malbihn. That miserable hundred grand, ain't nothing compared to the money I can get on talk shows, and book rights. Written by some ghostwriter of course! I can tell Baynes to shove his money where sun don't shine and a proctologist would have a tough time finding after that, I'm telling you," These were recurring statements, often uttered in growling tones as if there were someone other than himself, the burros and the rocks to hear.

The summer so-called monsoon thunderstorms gave him some temporary relief from the heat, but brought difficulties of their own. The water they brought was welcome to Malbihn and the burros alike, but the flash floods in the washes, ravines and arroyos brought sticking mud that made every step a trial with five pounds of muck sticking to boot and hoof. The storms were often preceded by wind driven blinding choking dust and when the quenching torrential rains finally came, thunder and lightning were often as not their bosom companion.

"Thunder is good, thunder is impressive, but lightning does the work," was a quote by Mark Twain that Malbihn never read, but he learned the truth of it up close and personal in early September, even as he was starting to head north into Utah, convinced he had scoured all of northern Arizona to no purpose. Utah would likely also be cooler he reckoned. Skirting north between Kanab, the Mormon town of Hilldale and short of Zion National Park there would be little chance of running into lots of people. He would be hard put to tell himself or anyone else, which was the stronger motivation, cooler weather or exploring new territory in his search.

Both burros were immune to the loud peals of thunder because they had experienced monsoon seasons many times. They stood in a pool of water that collected in a slightly flooded wash thankfully slaking their desperate thirst when lighting did its work. Even though the bolt hit a dead juniper stump fifty yards up the wash, both burros were electrocuted instantly. They almost looked thankful their misery was done.

Malbihn was furious. Even though their loads became much lighter through attrition, he knew he could only carry some of it. When he saw his shotgun sticking out from under the body of one, nearly covered with mud and water, he kicked the burro viciously as though the poor animal was to blame for his misfortune. His long rant was even more incoherent and disjointed.

"Damn dumb burro idiot, I told you to stay clear of water a hunnerd times, dint I?" Malbihn jumped up in down until he was covered with mud nearly to his knees. "Get up now. Get outta that damn muck you stupid shits. Who the hell is runnin' this outfit? You or me? Whaddya think I pay you for? I'm the one boffing the buffalo here."

The tirade went on for some time, attracting only the attention of two passing jackrabbits that immediately made themselves scarce, and a lone raven that paused from his meal of striped lizard. Falling finally silent, Malbihn regained enough composure to assess the losses and reckon on things he could do without. The shotgun was a total loss. Even if he had the tools to clean the action and barrel, the shells were in a side pouch on the burro and were now, not only under mud and water, but the carcass of the burro as well. Strong as he was, moving the body was beyond even his means. He extricated his sleeping bag, light canvas tent and a few other articles that would not overburden him and set them aside to dry in the now mocking sunshine. His determination to claim the money and find the damned *Kwi-ka-kikinee* was not only undiminished, it was stronger than ever, fueled by his rage and misfortune. No thought of turning back entered his head, although he had not completely lost his mind - yet.

Provisions had been running low for some time, and he was middling tired of eating dry goods occasionally augmented by jackrabbit, prickly pear cactus or a rare young javalina piglet. Malbihn proceeded to butcher the best parts of the two burros, jerking as much as he could with his remaining salt aided by the dry baking sun, saving out one big portion of the meatiest part of the ribs for supper. The meat was tough, rank, and lean, but to him it tasted almost as good as the rare t-bone he had the night he met J. Morrison Baynes.

NORTHWARD

September melded with October as Malbihn crossed the Utah border as planned. With the cooler air, his rapidly slipping sanity gained a brief footing. Even he was dimly aware of it. "Damn near went Looney Tunes down there. I betcha old *Kwi-ka-kikinee* don't like it neither in the heat. I'll find him up here for sure." This was to be one of his last rational thoughts.

The nights turned cold and his sun scolded skin and thinned blood complained bitterly. Thin blood notion is also a myth. Blood is blood, regardless of climate. The science of the matter is that the human body's capillaries, blood vessels that can carry red blood cells only single file, slowly migrate closer to the skin to more easily shed heat in warmer climates and reverse on colder ones. Malbihn, having spent years in hot Arizona had lost his Wisconsin tolerance for frigid temperatures. A high school dropout, he knew little about the biology of the thing. All he knew was his sleeping bag or rather what was left of it gave him little relief. Then cold suddenly became winter.

When the late October blizzard struck with 50 mile per hour winds, hail, and snow it shredded what was left of Malbihn's rapidly diminishing sanity. He wrapped the torn remnants of his tent around his shoulders, the now useless sleeping bag dropped into the snow as he plodded doggedly on leaning into the biting wind desperately seeking some form of shelter. The sweat stained Australian bush hat he habitually wore for years flew from his head in the gale, skipping rapidly away across the snow-covered ground as if to say "Goodbye." Freed from its constraint, his now shoulder length hair whipped around his head sometimes almost blinding his from what little he could see in the blowing snow.

Reaching a cliff side in a shallow ravine that blocked the swirling wind he reached into his tattered backpack, took out and ate the last of the jerked burro meat. It was rancid by now but that didn't matter much. As he chewed, he saw the envelope with the photos of *Kwi-ka-kikinee* in the bottom of his pack. Malbihn stared at them with burning intensity. The money, Baynes and fame were long forgotten but not the images of his quarry and obsession. Looking up during a brief lull in the storm, he espied a small cave on the opposite side of the ravine. "Shelter," was the last utterance of human language that came from his cracked lips. The precious photos dropped from his numbed fingers into the snow. The backpack, now useless was left where it lay. Staggering and half-running he crossed over and peered into the cave. It was dark and just large enough for him to crawl in. As he did, he caught a faint odor of animal and more importantly, a faint feeling of warmth. About four feet in the cave ended. He could hear the rustling of twigs and the animal smell increased.

Finally, his stinging eyes adjusted to the gloom and he saw the cause of all three crude sensory observations. Wriggling in a hollow of twigs and brush were two bobcat cubs. Their eyes glowed cat-like as he approached but they were more curious than alarmed. Without thinking, Malbihn gathered them in his arms, curled up with them and shared the combined warmth of all three bodies. Within a few minutes

Although, there was some playful purring, sniffing and licking all three dozed off. About an hour later, he was woken by a spitting guttural hiss from the entrance of the cave. The mother bobcat had returned with it's prey, a small jackrabbit. The carcass was now at her feet, nourishment for her and her cubs forgotten, amidst the protective urge of the bobcat. Despite the size disparity between her and Malbihn, motherly instinct took over and she sprang to the attack. Grasping her by the throat with one hand, Malbihn ignored the rending claws as he alternately choked the life out of his antagonist while raining savage blows on her. Finally seizing a rock, he ended the battle with a skull-crunching blow to her head. Bleeding and exhausted, his scant covering further shredded, he retreated to the rear of the cave, curled up and fell asleep.

When he awoke, the cubs had nibbled at the jackrabbit and were whining and nuzzling their mother. Apparently, they felt no rancor toward Malbihn, because when they saw him moving they approached without fear and rubbed up against his thigh. Life and death struggles in the wild are accepted as natural by the creatures that are surrounded by this fact. Malbihn, now thoroughly a semi-savage beast himself, petted the cubs, then used a sharp rock to tear open the mother bobcat and proceeded to start eating her raw. As he did this, his long hair kept falling in front of his face, so he fashioned a thong from the bobcat's gut by twisting it and wrapped it around his forehead. The unlikely trio lived in the cave for over two months. Food was scarce, but they managed to survive on packrats, mice, juniper berries, prickly pear cacti and edible roots that Malbihn dug up. The cubs, while not yet full-grown, had long since been weaned and one day when a rabbit den was discovered that he could not reach into, the cats burrowed in and killed the rabbits. When they emerged, one was holding a rabbit in his mouth and dropped it at Malbihn's feet.

MIGRATION

In early February during a warm spell, they began to migrate south. As they did, Malbihn stumbled across his discarded pack. Idly rummaging through it like the wild animal he now was, he accidentally nicked a finger on his old hunting knife, once gleaming and sharp, now rusted and dull but still with a fairly sharp point. He stuffed it in the makeshift belt wrap he fashioned from what was left of the covering he still had from his tent. Two days later, he used to kill a small antelope, he ambushed from the branches of a small tree.

The cubs were now nearly full grown so the trio ate better and had little fear of being caught off guard by casual hikers, hunters or similar migrants. It would be hard to determine if they considered themselves friends or travel companions for convenience. Malbihn had few softer sentiments in his past life, but it was quite possible that the bobcats felt some familial affection for their surrogate parent. Nonetheless the worked well as a team and slept with each other every night. Hardship, privation and his now primitive life further deteriorated Malbihn's already primitive mentality. When he spoke, it was in monosyllables and he continually babbled *Kwi-ka-kikinee, Kwi-ka-kikinee, Kwi-ka-kikinee,* as though to reinforce his obsession. The few occasional hikers he saw he shunned, possibly through fear, but more likely an aversion to civilized beings. Occasionally, "will find, no stop, get him," or "soon find," passed his lips. His communication with the twin bobcats was mostly by hissing sounds, high- pitched shrill cries or hand signals that they eventually all came to understand.

Only once, there was a confrontation with a fellow human being. They were approaching once again the hills of the Sanup plateau when they came upon a tiny ramshackle building nestled against some boulders adjacent to a shallow arroyo. A rusted hulk of a truck on flat tires stood drunkenly beside it. Malbihn saw the smoke from the cabin wood stove and was about to circle wide of the beat up shack when he saw it's occupant emerge to find a place to urinate. The man was nearly naked, long hair and beard covering most of his chest, neck and shoulders. Maibihn's eyes glittered and a surge of energy bust through his limbs. "*Kwi-ka-kikinee,*" he muttered continually as he ran toward the shack. A clattering of a rock only thirty yards away was the first warning the hermit heard before Malbihn soon stood directly in front of him, hands clenching and releasing, glassy eyes now mere slits. Directly behind the frightening apparition Malbihn presented, stood the two nearly adult bobcats.

"*Kwi-ka-kikinee, Kwi-ka-kikinee,*" Malbihn cried.

The man muttered, "What the hell," turned and bolted for the open door. Malbihn was right on his heels. Grabbing a shotgun the man tried to turn on his pursuer, but it was ripped from his hands as he squeezed the trigger and the blast simply put another hole in the roof of the shack.

Glowering at the prostrate man, Malbihn glanced around the interior. A filthy cot, woodstove, cook pots and a few other household possessions immediately convinced him that this wild man was not *Kwi-ka-kikinee.* As he bludgeoned the hermit to death with the butt of the shotgun, he muttered angrily, "not *Kwi-ka-kikinee,* me find, not him, you not *Kwi- ka-kikinee!*" The stock of the shotgun was splintered beyond redemption and Malbihn was heaving and sweating as he exited the cabin, not knowing he had just murdered Jasper Bemis, a harmless homeless hermit. It is quite possible that the untransformed Malbihn would have felt no more remorse than he did when he killed the old Indian some time past in the distant recesses of his memory. The bobcats entered Jasper's remote retreat and contemplated a meal.

Malbihn and his wild companions continued their aimless migration south toward the Colorado River and the Hualapai Indian Reservation. The trails they followed seemed vaguely familiar to Malbihn, but his now jumbled mind did not know why nor did he care. There was no hurry. The bobcats gave it no thought either. Following a descending trail into the lower end of the canyon, they ascended near the Reservation Lodge where Malbihn had bid a dour adieu to his customers over a year before. Sheltering from sight in a thick stand of trees, he saw a group of well provided for hikers conversing with an Indian guide. Although he was in easy earshot of the conversation, he understood none of it. The Indian seem distantly familiar but that was all.

J. MORRISON BAYNES

"Great trip, and worth every penny," one man said to Eah Walla the guide. I was on the same trip a year or two ago with your former employer Karl Malbihn. You drove my Land Rover down from Utah if I recall. He was a sour son of a bitch and your knowledge of the native culture is so much better. If you don't mind me asking, I notice you dress differently than your fellows and your name is very different too. Aren't you from this tribe?"

"You are very observant Mr. Harder. I married into the Hualapai Tribe four years ago. I am a Taos Pueblo Indian from New Mexico. I am named after my great grandfather whose name meant Corn Medicine. I was happy to be your guide and appreciate very much your generous gratuity. And your compliments. I will share the money with the drivers who should be here any minute. Are you staying at the lodge?"

"Yes, I'm also anxious to send an e-mail to an old friend of mine who has a business down in Peach Springs. How's the internet connection?"

"You should have no problem Mr. Harder, we upgraded the system just six months or so ago." replied Eah Walla. "Much better than smoke signals you will find." The two shared a chuckle and parted company.

The phone rang in George Caruthers real estate office in Peach Springs. He thought it unusual because it was on the landline he seldom used and was even considering giving up to save money. Cell phones were now the norm and he could hardly remember the last time the thing had actually rung, but he knew who the caller probably was.

"Have you had any word from, or about Malbihn?" This was the immediate question after George said hello.

"Nothing, J.M. but I got an e-mail from Bill Harder at the Hualapai Reservation about an hour ago that you might be very interested in," George replied. "I'll forward it to you in a few minutes. It doesn't have anything to do with that surly Malbihn guy, but you'll want to see the attachments. Another supposed sighting of the *Kwi-ka Kikanee* myth you're so keen on."

***

Seventeen minutes later in Manhattan, J. Morrison Baynes downloaded the digital photos Caruthers forwarded and pulled them up immediately to view on the large flat screen monitor that sat on his polished mahogany desk.

"I suppose I wasted the money I spent on Malbihn," he mused aloud as he put on his glasses to view the photos. One of the black and white photos, copies of which he had supplied Malbihn, was framed and sitting next to his computer. Other than the fact that the photo on the screen was high-resolution digital color, complete with a time and date code, the images were very similar with a few small details of difference. The mountain background was the same as was the shaggy creature including the ragged canvas like clothing but there appeared to be a hilt of a knife protruding from it's waist band and instead of the lone wolf, a pair of bobcats stood next to him. One nearly touching his left leg.

Baynes started to consider whom else he might engage to track the thing when his eye caught a detail his first glance missed. Zooming in on the photo, he saw a small tattoo on the creature's wrist. It was a silhouette looking much like the state of Wisconsin, albeit with a ragged scar cutting across it. Below it were the letters KM/FU.

J. Morrison Baynes shut down his computer, went over to the credenza put some ice in a tall glass from an ice bucket and poured in a generous amount of expensive, unblended Scotch Whiskey.

By Robert Vonkepner

Playing Games

By

Clint Stutts

He'd been in a lot of rooms like this before, and this one was no different than any of the others. The walls had that dingy yellow color that could only be attributed to the thousands, or perhaps millions, of cigarettes that had been smoked in here before. The door was solid steel, no little window for anyone to look through. The table was about six by three, solid steel.

The chairs were the uncomfortable kind, almost certainly manufactured to make people want to get out of them as soon as they sat down. And of course there was the one way glass on one side of the room, where "big brother" could listen to what was said and see every expression on the face of the person being interrogated. Jase Riza had been in a lot of these rooms in his 52 years, and every time it had been for a good reason, but not this time. This time he was innocent, and by God he wasn't going to admit to anything, no matter how hard they leaned on him.

The twenty-four years of total prison time he had served in his life had been enough for him, and for the last two years since he'd gotten out, he had been living straight for the first time in his miserable life. He'd been sent up for armed robbery three times, and the last stint he'd spent in prison was enough for him. And now they were trying to pin a murder on him. How quaint he thought.

The solid steel door opened, and a well-dressed man wearing Ray-Ban sunglasses walked in. His face was expressionless, his hair was slicked back, and his suit was extremely well kept, no wrinkles at all. He had in his hand what Jase could only guess was his file, which contained everything Jase had ever done that had landed him in police custody. "Mr. Well Dressed Guy" shut the door, and then stood there and stared at Jase. Jase couldn't see "Mr. Well Dressed Guy's" eyes, but he could sense something bad emanating from them.

Finally, he walked to the chair opposite Jase, and sat down. The file he had in his hand was placed on the table in front of him, and "Mr. Well Dressed Guy" slowly unwound the string that was holding the file closed. Jase chose to break the silence first.

"So, are we gonna sit here forever while you flip through my file, or are we gonna get this over with?"

The man looked up from the file, and took his sunglasses off to reveal the most chilling pair of eyes Jase had ever seen. The look coming from those eyes was one that said, "I will kill you if you so much as look at me in a way that pisses me off." He folded the sunglasses up and slipped them into the front pocket of his coat.

"I'm Detective Thompson, and I'll be handling this case today. I'm done flipping through your file, so yes, we can get this over with." Thompson cracked a smile. This made Jase feel as though he was enjoying his job, and maybe actually looked forward to coming to work every day and busting scumbags like him.

"I'm not going to lie to you Mr. Riza," Thompson continued, "you're in a lot of trouble this time. It seems you've graduated from armed robbery and decided to go all the way to murder. I'd like to know why, if you don't mind."

"I didn't kill that lady. I've never seen her before in my life. All I know is, I got picked up when I was walking' home from the gas station on the corner. The cops who picked me up said I killed a lady named Carol Dyson. It was news to me."

Thompson didn't look satisfied. "Mr. Riza, I'm not here to play games. All I want is for you to own up to what you did. I'm looking for one answer from you. If you sit here and deny everything, we're both going to be here a very long time. I know you killed this woman. We've got two witnesses who claim that a man matching your description attempted to rob the station, and in the course of that robbery shot and killed Mrs. Dyson. If you'll just confess to what we both know you did, you may get a life sentence instead of the death penalty. I can have a talk with the D.A. and arrange that for you. What do you say to that, Mr. Riza?"

Jase was not intimidated. Every interrogator he'd ever dealt with was an asshole, and this guy was playing the part like a pro.

"Well, Mr. Thompson, I got all the time in the world. You got no evidence to convict me of anything. Yeah, I was at the station, but all I did was buy some cigs, and---"

Thompson slammed his hand down on the table…hard. It was so sudden and so loud that Jase let a small cry escape his mouth.

"Mr. Riza, I told you I'm not here to play games, but it seems you *insist* on playing games. So I've got one for you. It's called Russian Roulette."

Jase thought he was kidding until the bastard produced a .38 revolver from his ankle holster and began removing all the bullets except one. He put the bullets in his right coat pocket. Thompson gave the cylinder a good spin and snapped it shut, just like in the movies. Except this wasn't a damn movie.

"Detective Thompson, I don't think---," Jase began, but Thompson already had the gun to his own head and

pulled the trigger. A dry 'click' sound followed no shot.
Thank God. Jase had an idea this guy had some serious
mental problems.

Thompson gave the cylinder a spin again and
placed the gun in front of Jase. "It's your turn now. You
wanted to play games, you got your wish," said
Thompson.

"If you think I'm gonna put that gun to my head
and pull the trigger, you're crazy!" said Jase.

"Maybe I'm crazy, maybe I'm not. It really doesn't
matter, Mr. Riza. What matters is that you are going to
put that gun to your head and pull the trigger. You'll do
it, because if you don't, I'll just blow your head off
anyway." With that said, Thompson pulled what looked
like a .45 caliber semi-automatic pistol from his shoulder
holster.

"Play the game, or I finish it right now," said
Thompson.

Jase slowly reached for the gun, trying to think of
something he could do to get out of the mess he was in. It
was obvious Thompson was mental, and probably
wanted to kill him anyway. It was even more obvious
that no one was behind the one way glass. If someone
had been behind there, they'd have stopped this thing as
soon as Thompson pulled his gun. If he screamed, it was
a sure thing he'd be shot. Yes, something was wrong
here, and if somebody didn't do something quick, things
were going to get messy. He Thought to himself *You're all
by yourself, old buddy. Just you and Mr. Happy Crappy.*

The gun was in Jase's hands now, and the cold grip
sent a chill up his spine. He thought of turning the gun

on Thompson and taking a chance that the bullet was in the right chamber, but he thought better of it. If he wasn't quick enough Thompson would just shoot him where he sat.   Plus, there was a very low chance, one in six that the bullet would be in the right place. He put the gun to his head, said a prayer to the God he never paid attention to, and pulled the trigger. The dry 'click' sound again and he had a thought in the back of his mind *Oh, can you say thankya Gawd, can I get praise Jeeezus!*

Thompson smiled and grabbed the gun from Jase. With the cylinder spun again, he put the gun to his own head again, and pulled the trigger. He lucked out again, but he was frowning. "This could take forever," he said. "I think we need to make this more challenging." He then reached into his coat pocket and retrieved two more bullets. Jase could see that he was putting the bullets in every other chamber. Not good.

"Here ya go, Riza. Your turn," said Thompson. Jase had to think of something, and quick. The game just got a lot scarier.

"I don't think it's fair that I have to be the first one to try it with three bullets. I think---"

"I don't care what you think, Riza. You can either play the game, or I can win by forfeit, and I guess you know what that means." Jase didn't want to play anymore; he didn't want to play to begin with. He'd been lucky the first time, but the second time was likely to either kill him, or make him a vegetable. Maybe if he confessed it would end the game. It couldn't hurt to try. The confession obviously wasn't going to be witnessed by anyone, and so wouldn't be admissible in court. That much he knew.

"Mr. Thompson, I'd like to confess now. I really don't want to play games with you. I know how valuable your time is and you just want to do your job." Oh, he was sucking up the best he could now. "I really did kill that woman, and I deserve what the courts give me for the crime."

"That's lovely Mr. Riza, but I still want to play the game. I think it's quite amusing. Now take the gun and have your turn."

Jase took it reluctantly. He put it to his head and held it there for a moment. Thompson looked at him intensely. Jase's bladder let go and warm urine ran down his right leg. Thompson heard it running on the floor and smiled. Jase pulled the trigger and was still alive. The smile on Thompson's face faded to an angry sneer.

"You're pretty lucky, Riza," he said. "You're probably thinking I'll be the one to run out of luck first, but I've got a surprise for you. Since I'm the one in charge here, I get to change the rules whenever the hell I want to." Thompson opened the cylinder and took out the two bullets he had loaded into the gun earlier. He spun the cylinder, snapped it shut, and put the gun to his head again.

"Why are you even doing this?" Jase asked him. "You're still risking your life, even with one bullet. What makes you so sure you won't kill yourself the next time you pull that trigger?" Thompson lowered the gun and looked solemnly at Jase.

"Like I said, it doesn't matter. Whether you die or I die, it doesn't matter to me," said Thompson. Jase could see Thompson's face change as he said these words. He had gone from insane to somber in five seconds flat.

Thompson put the gun back to his head and pulled the trigger. This time, there wasn't a dry 'click'. This time, the gun went off and blew the opposite side of Thompson's head wide open. Blood sprayed onto the table in front of Jase. All he could do was look at it, terrified. No words, no screams could escape his mouth. It was as if the world had suddenly run out of air and Jase felt suffocated.

The hand Thompson used to fire the gun, his right hand, flopped down and the gun hit the floor with a dull thunk. Thompson's eyes were filled with shock, or perhaps it wasn't shock. It could have been just a generic look people get when they shoot themselves in the head. Jase didn't really know. What Jase did know was that Thompson wasn't dead. He wasn't falling to the floor or slumping over the table like most head shot victims would. His left hand still held the other pistol, the one with a full clip, and that hand was slowly sliding the gun toward Jase. He couldn't pick it up, but he could slide it just fine, it seemed. Jase, frozen to his chair, frozen in time, could only watch.

He could hear voices outside the door screaming, "Shot fired! Shot fired! Check your weapons, check your prisoners! Where'd it come from?"

Blood was gushing from the massive wound on Thompson's head. *My brain is working,* Jase thought, *but I can't move. All I have to do is move. He isn't in the best shape now and he Can't catch me if I run. He can't even follow me with the gun very well. Just move, damnit. Move. Move. MOVE!*

Jase moved. He did the only thing that came to mind, he toppled his chair and himself onto one side, and found himself on the floor. As he fell, Thompson managed to squeeze off a shot. It hit the stone wall behind Jase and bits of the wall sprayed to the floor. *That could have been me*, Jase thought.

Before another shot was fired, a street cop and several plainclothes detectives burst through the door.

"FREEZE!" one of the detectives screamed. As they digested the scene before them, another detective blurted, "Christ, its Dyson! What the hell is he even doing here?" This one stepped forward and grabbed the gun away from Thompson, who was still sitting in his chair bleeding all over himself. The street cop yelled for someone to call an ambulance, but Jase was pretty sure it would end up hauling a dead body to the morgue.

Suddenly, things began making sense to Jase. Thompson was really Dyson, as in possibly the husband of one Carol Dyson. He was finally able to speak. "This guy almost killed me! He had me playing Russian Roulette with him! What the hell kind of police station are you guys running here, anyway?"

"We're terribly sorry Mr. Riza. I'm Detective Matson, and I want you to know this situation is now under control."

"That's nice to hear, Detective," Jase replied, as the two other detectives picked him up off the floor. "Could you fill me in on why the hell this guy tried to kill me?

You called him Dyson, but he identified himself as Thompson when he came in here."

Matson began to explain, but two paramedics arrived and cut him short. Thompson/Dyson was pronounced dead at the scene. Matson began again, "Apparently, Dyson suffered a breakdown this morning when his wife was shot and killed at the robbery you're a suspect in. He wasn't even supposed to be here; he was on bereavement leave. The detective assigned to your case was actually Detective Juarez, but we found him in a supply closet a few minutes ago. Dyson had knocked him silly with the butt of his gun. But as I said before, we're terribly sorry about what happened. Now Mr. Riza, we still have the issue of your involvement in this morning's robbery to discuss."

New Thoughts on Patsy Cline and Living

by

Amanda Connor

So many versions of her existed, I don't think she ever settled on one. People called her the Patsy Cline of Posey County. I called her my mother, Momma, and Della Louise when I was mad. Others called her a whore. Momma, she called herself a legend on the good days and a failure on the bad days.

A cedar box containing her ashes sits buckled in on the passenger seat of my truck. Now, my mother, at just

42 years old, is reduced to one box. I keep glancing over to the box uncomfortable in its presence.

Before she died, Momma asked me to go to the Smoky Mountains with my sister, Dakota and spread her ashes. She said it would help us. Maybe bring us closer again, like we used to be.

She said, "When you go there on vacation with my grandbabies, I'll already be there, waiting for you."

A few years ago, we went on vacation there, Momma, Dakota, and I. It was the first and the last vacation, we ever took together just the three of us. She loved it there. Said it was "peaceful" and called it "God's country." Dakota complained the whole time. I tested out the wineries and kept us stocked up on the best tasting wines. We all had fun though.

I can almost hear Momma's loud laugh that carried for miles. The vivacious Della Louise with red lips and romantic arched eyebrows, dark hair and dark eyes. Wider eyed than Patsy Cline and less in control of herself. Nevertheless, the woman drew in attention and turned all eyes on her by simply sauntering on stage and saying, "Hello." When she opened her mouth to sing, people held their breath, afraid to disrupt the sound. Under her attention, a person felt like the most important person thing in the world, no matter how fleeting the moment. If a person was lucky enough to catch her attention, they basked in its glow.

Then, there were those days, where it seemed she lost contact with herself and the world. She seemed despondent and desperate. Those days, she hid mostly locked behind her bedroom door with blinds drawn, the lights out, and the radio playing low.

*

At work today, the lady with the fake happy voice called me. I instantly recognized her. She's the tall lady with the short blonde hair and the painted-on smile that walked us through the process of Momma's funeral and cremation, the morning after she died. Lisa Grayson the Assistant Director of Grayson Funeral Home, wife of Tom Grayson owner. The Grayson family had owned the funeral home as far back as my great grandmother's mother's funeral. Our families knew each other. Lisa went to school with my mother. She knew Momma as the pretty one who got knocked up in their senior year and she had a full scholarship to some music school. She also knew my Momma as the woman with the voice that got too drink to perform most nights at Jack's. Of course, most of the old families in this town know who's who and what's what in a town this size.

If anyone knows the real dirt in families, though, it is the funeral home family in a town. They not only deal with the dead, they deal with the family and all the scandal that come with it. This family member is mad at that one or sleeping with that one and they can't be in the funeral home at the same time. Or so and so is banned because he stole Grandpa's guns. Then there's the tragedies where death is sudden and unexpected the ones that are emotional wrecks. The ones that stick together, the ones with the money and without, and the ones with friends and without.

She had a whine to her voice, one that led you to believe you were an irritant she quickly needed to rid herself of.

"Hello. Is this Amber?" She didn't give me time to answer. "Your mother's cremains came in today. When will you come and pick them up?"

The word "cremains" bothered me. It didn't feel real, felt like some made up word used in a movie or cartoon.

"I'll be in later today. I'm at work right now so I—" "That'll be fine. We close at five. Have a nice day." I could hear her hang up before I had a chance to say thank her.

I didn't trust the woman after the way she treated me when we were planning Momma's funeral. She didn't really say or do anything. It was the way she made me feel smaller than her, even when she was smiling I could see her eyes looking down at me.

When my sister Dakota and I went to go plan Momma's funeral, it was a circus. My sister Dakota was all hopped up on the meth just twitching and picking imaginary lint off her legs, her son Dylan climbed over the chairs.

Dakota yelled, "I'm gonna spank your little ass if you don't sit down. Don't you understand your mamaw is dead. God!"

I grabbed him up, gave her a sideways glance, and put him on my lap. She announced to the room she was going to go smoke a cigarette to compose herself because she's endured "all she could handle."

The woman smiled and kept on talking. She got into the finances of it all and asked me three times throughout her coverage of the costs if I understood they had to have so much upfront before anything is done. I told her I did each time. The last time she asked I told her it would be paid in full that Momma had life insurance. She was taken back that my mother had life insurance. I guess she figured my mother a savage that didn't have such things.

She quickly regained her composure and said, "Well, good."

The woman even tried to talk me out of getting flowers for my mother's casket since she would be cremated after the one day of open visitation.

"It's completely up to you…but others will probably send a few flowers and things. Since she'll be cremated… well, there will be no burial service. No real need for flowers. So if I was concerned about costs, I wouldn't worry about flowers. They can be pretty expensive. But that's just my opinion."

"I'm not concerned about costs ma'am," I said.

I didn't' want to leave my mother there with her any longer than I had to. I didn't want to keep Momma waiting either. I didn't want her to be there on some shelf alone, or worse among other left behind "cremains." Are there "cremains" left there at the place never to be retrieved by anyone who cared? If I didn't go to get her, no one would. Dakota might eventually go get her, once someone finally got in contact with her. She moved around so much it was hard to get in contact with her to tell her Momma had passed.

*

I left my office in the west wing of the mansion and went downstairs through the Gallery to my boss's office to let him know I was leaving early. He's seventy and has a Ph.D. in philosophy, among several other degrees. Momma said he came from "old money" which means "his shit doesn't stink."' He likes to be called Dr. Walters. He's an overgrown child of a man with gray hair, a large red-faced, and a god complex, who regularly busts staplers and phones or really anything in his sight when something goes wrong with his precious "Plan," which includes a nine-hundred-page book entitled *New Thoughts on Achieving a State of Equilibrium* and a series of lectures to be hosted by him at his sprawling mansion in serious need of repair.

*

I can't help but feel loyal to him though. When Momma got sick, he let me work mostly from home and still paid me my full-time pay. We wouldn't have been able to get by without that money.

He calls me his "apprentice." He likes the word and uses it frequently. Maybe he thinks it makes the job more desirable somehow and justifies the ridiculously low wages he pays me. Really the word is completely out of context for the work that I do which is to write what he tells me to and find recruits for his lectures he's planning. An apprentice learns from a skilled tradesman.

Dr. Walters is a very intelligent man, but he is so isolated from the real world that he doesn't realize his New Thoughts, ideas that were groundbreaking and new when he was popular in the 1970's, are not new anymore. I have seen some of the things he discusses in his books talked about on various blogs and numerous books. The only difference is the way it's dressed up. I only know this because I've worn out the self-help section of the bookstore and the web trying to fix me and my family. Most self-help theories and practices can be traced back to philosophy and psychology.

So I make a good fit for Dr. Walters. I applied online and got hired right after the interview. I think the only reason he hired me though, is because I had a Master's degree and I'm a good listener. He doesn't like to be interrupted, although he wasn't very pleased when he noted that I studied psychology. He thought philosophy to be much more superior.

A B C D E F
16 21 40 46 60 Eagles
Tri-bugs
OPEN ZONE
Angled square housing
N6
Basic Ser
Basic Ser
Basic Ser
Basic Ser
Basic Ser
Basic Ser
Basic Ser
Bas
Bas
Bas
Bas
Z41
60
N5
Mounting Plate
NIVELO 4 IMPLIED
Lost Zone
7-30-2016
Extended diffuser
NIVELO 3
Splayed cone exhaust
NIV 2
Sprocket
Secondary diffuser
Nivl
A63
150 Eagles
BASE
BASE SERVICE PACKAGE

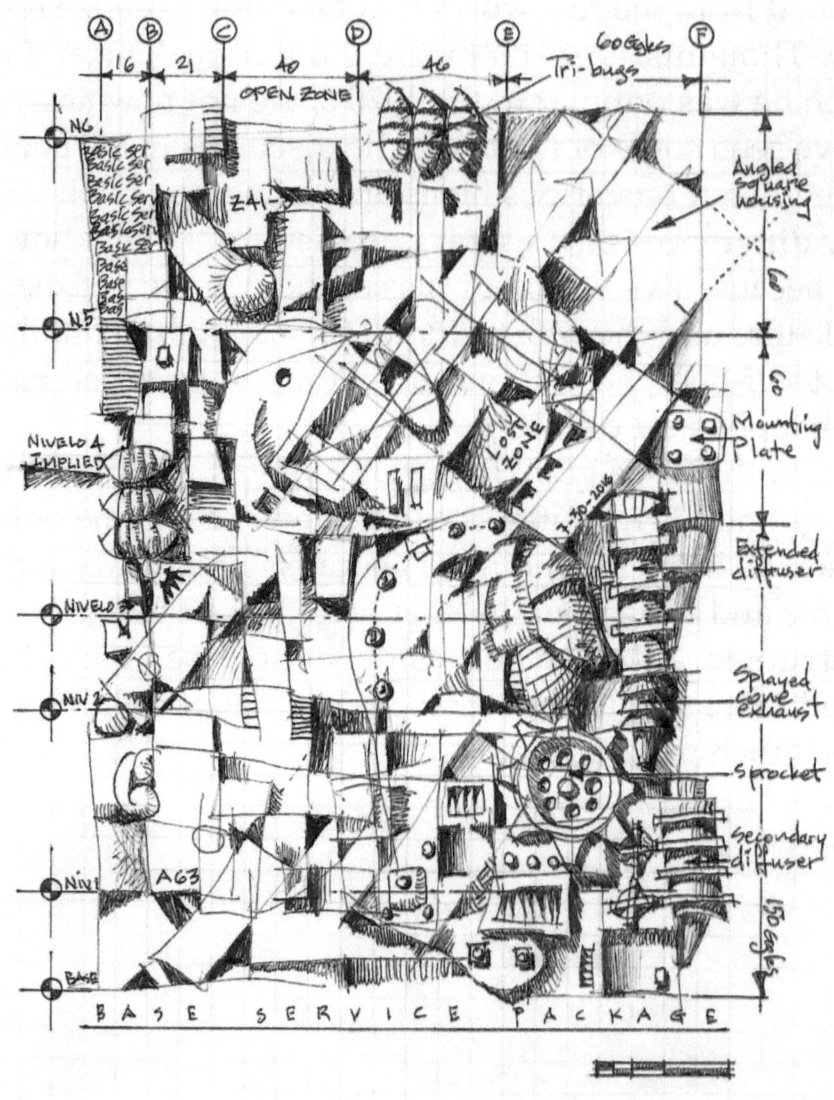

By Floater

HUBRIS

By

Ellen Drebin

What price fame? How far would you bend your ethics to hold onto the power that fame entails.? What follows is the story of two men who found out.

A receptionist covering the front desk for a resort area physician turned to her boss and asked, "Am I the only one seeing double?"

"What do you mean?"

"That patient you just saw... you didn't notice how much he looked like the guy who was in yesterday?"

"Which one?"

She fiddles with the computer in front of her. "Tom Bradford."

"You think Bradford looks like Edward Wong?"

"A dead ringer, boss. Good looking guys and they're the same age. I checked."

"Watch out with the sleuthing, Lisa. Their files are confidential."

"Okay, I will from now on. But I already looked. They're from completely different places....but they were here to see you with the same complaint."

"Interesting."

"Could you ask them if they're adopted?"

"Bradford and Wong? No way"

She sighs. "Okay, boss. My Dad always said I was too nosy."

As soon as he's gone back to his office, she calls her best friend. "Hey, Stacy, what's your take on this? You know how strong I've always been on facial recognition."

"True. You're amazing in that regard."

"Yeah, wish it were a marketable skill. Anyway, there are two guys coming into this office who are identical. They're the same age, but they come from different places."

"Let it go, Lis. Don't be a jerk... like when you fixed your cousin up with a guy who had just mistreated her on Tinder."

"Well, I scheduled their follow-up visits for the same day and time."

"Holy smoke If being a busy body is a crime, you're the prime example."

The next time Tom Bradford comes to the office, Lisa delays him at her desk ...until Edward Wong walks in. They gape at each other.

Edward Wong is more reticent but Tom Bradford blurts out, "May I ask your name?"

"Edward Wong. And yours?"

"Tom Bradford. I'm an engineer from Seattle."

"I'm an engineer from Vancouver."

"Were you born there?"

"No, in China."

For a few moments. There's silence as the mental wheels spin. Both men are extremely bright but it's Ed Wong, who has the background to get suspicious first. He asks Tom, "Do you know both of your parents?"

"Only my late Dad. He was career military."

"Was he ever stationed in China?"

"Yes. A long time ago."

"About when you were born?"

Growing pale, Tom nods.

"The one child policy."

"Why do you bring that up?"

"Because I don't know my father."

"What are you getting at?"

"It's pure speculation, of course, but could we have been twins?"

"Holy smoke"

The two bright men, with life experiences that are world's apart, both suddenly sense that certain unspoken mysterious holes in their lives may finally becoming filled in. Tentatively, they reach out and shake hands.

"Nice to meet you," Tom says inadequately.

"Same here," Ed replies, bowing slightly.

The following day, Tom meets with his father's estate lawyer, Eli Green, and asks, "Did my Dad ever tell you anything about having another son?"

Eli looks at him curiously. "No, but he did insist on some rather oblique wording in his will that I couldn't fathom. Why do you ask?"

"I met a man yesterday who looks just like me....I mean really identical."

"Where?"

"At a doctor's office. This other guy and I are nothing alike, I'm sure, because he was raised in China. He was likely poor and he may have been faced with prejudice against Amerasians."

Eli's face is impassive. "What's your conjecture?"

"My lookalike thought that, If my father fell in love with his mother...a Chinese national... they could have freaked out about the one child policy when she had twins."

"So... your Dad could have brought you here. What did your father ever tell you about your mother?"

"He was evasive...got very military whenever I brought it up. Said he loved her very much but that a political situation made the relationship impossible... so we just had to deal with it. We were two guys on our own."

"Interesting. So what do you want from me, Tom?""

"To sort out the legal ramifications. My father's years in the defense industry after his retirement from the military were profitable."

"That's true."

"How does this new development affect his estate.

Eli ponders the precedents involved for a few minutes. He looks at Tom. "What would mean more to you.... money or having a brother?"

"I think having a brother. I was so lonely growing up." Then, in a completely unexpected change of subject, Tom asks, "Do you think my eyes look Asian?"

"Perhaps a bit more than your father's. Your hair is certainly darker. But I've always thought you were both unusually handsome men." Eli's glances up. "Does this other man have kids?"

Tom's hand flies to his forehead. "Geez, I have no idea. Why?"

"Well, it could be important. Say he's got eight kids. The way your Dad
worded the will, "I bequeath to my heirs equally," his estate would have to be split ten ways."

"Holy shit " They stare at each other. Then, laughing, Tom takes a tube from his pocket and jokes, "Could I borrow some of your spit to send in for the DNA test?"

"Hey, seriously, raised as an only child, you have been a bit spoiled."

"But I want to get to know my brother."

And so a modern fairy tale began. The initial period of getting acquainted was euphoric. Both men felt a sense of connection that they had never had with any friend before. There was a spring in their steps as they experienced boundless energy. The special communication said to exist between twins soon developed. They could predict each other's reactions. Life was good.

Before a year had passed, Tom talked Ed into relocating to Seattle. Engineers with different specialties, they decided to use their joint inheritance to fund a start-up that would combine Tom's skill in robotics with Ed's in the fast-moving field of Artificial Intelligence. Both raced to work each morning with excitement and a feeling of new possibilities. They decided to produce AI-powered, robotic valets for doing household chores, solving problems and even offering companionship.

Startups in Japan were doing similar creative things. But theirs was an immediate hit. Tom's wife, a marketing/PR pro with great connections, introduced it as no more threatening than a beloved pet... and equally good for one's safety and mental health.

Success suited the brothers well and they learned fast. Before long, both were living in breathtaking homes, driving high end cars, dining often in five star restaurants and becoming generous philanthropists. Magazines loved doing covers of the two photogenic twins who were impossible to tell apart.

Within a few years, talk began among political backers that one of them should run for public office. They decided it should be Tom as he was native born. They soon announced his candidacy and the campaign attracted generous donations.

Tom was so well-known and personable that he seemed unbeatable, An attractive young groupie came to work in his campaign office and, before long, started to flirt with him. A few times when they were alone there, she came on to him. It may not have been his idea but she was fresh-faced and young and worshipped him. One night, they moved to his private office in back and nature took its course. He tried to keep from getting too involved... until she told him she was pregnant and demanded that he leave his wife and marry her. When he refused, she grabbed her coat and told him she was heading to the newspaper office across the river to spill the beans.

Days later, a supermarket tabloid prints a photo that appears to show a scuffle with Tom pushing her off the bridge.. . whether by intent or accident. Someone in the vicinity at the time caught the moment on his cell phone camera. Cable T.V. shows and late night comics are on it endlessly and mercilessly. They now can't seem to get enough of humiliating and taking down a star whom they had previously helped make.

Tom is devastated. Ambition and the lust for power have taken hold of him. He is like Icarus flying too close to the sun. From the even tempered, modest engineer he had once been, he has become a wealthy, entitled celebrity. He is now addicted to stardom. He has tasted fame and he can't let go.

Racking his brain, he sees only one possible way to still win and preserve his place in the limelight. So, that very day, he creates anonymous bots that insist the photo was actually of Ed.

An outraged Ed rushes over the following morning while Tom is still in the shower. When Tom saunters into the room without a care in the world, Ed asks, "Where does this end? 'Confucius say, 'When anger erupts, consider the consequences.'"

"I have, "Tom replies confidently. "You've got to take the long view here. No jury could convict either of us 'beyond a shadow of a doubt.' I'm certain you're safe."

"But you're not," Ed says. "Your mother would be ashamed of you and, in your hubris, you've overlooked the superior, investigative skills of artificial intelligence.”

“What are you talking about?”

“AI has already analyzed the data on your Fiitbit.”

“How the hell could you get your hands on that?”

“I had your personal valet fetch it for me and I transmitted the data to the police. You underestimated how great our product is, Tom.”

It was that second misplaced apostrophe that finally pushed Dan over the edge...

Check out more cartoons like this….
www.inkygirl.com

From Birth I Knew
My Life Wouldn't

By
Dytania Johnson

From birth I knew my life wouldn't be an easy one, for as I lay in the hospital nursery, surrounded by pink and white striped blankets, twenty babies filled the room and I was the only boy. Yes, me! What are the odds that from so many different cries, that I couldn't hear myself. Through it all, I knew it was a lifelong training for creating a meeting of the masses, for world domination.

Wait! What do you know?! Another male figure who people around me call dad, daddy, pops, and my old man. Nonetheless, as months went by, the less of him I see, periodically poking his face in with mom down his throat, saying, "You're a sorry good for nothing buggar." The stress or cowardness of responsibility, is a label given to those who were supposed to raise me to become the man I should be. Or was it a constant put down? The high pitched screams that woke me up while I was in slumber - who's to blame, I wondered. Wasn't he supposed to be mentally stronger for his only son? Well, that was the last I saw of him. I was often left in my mom's care, and with my uncles who had kids of their own. I was also left with the guys who were way older than I was, but never stuck around to inflict some type of manly characteristic in me, because of their not-so-legal backgrounds - but that's an entirely different story.

It was a day less than my second birthday, when I noticed that my mom's stomach had been growing bigger as time went by. The adult beverage of choice was catching up with her, and after listening closely to the recent whispers, I came to believe that a sibling was coming soon. Oh God, could it be a brother? It was the ultimate birthday gift, and the idea alone was barely keeping my head afloat. I could feel myself drowning in estrogen and I couldn't wait to see how life would change. Even though I haven't really lived, standing over me were the towering giants who were guarding me. They were followers of Athena herself, and there were so many women. They were hand pointing at me; don't do this, don't do that, and teaching me the first steps to training the male species to do their bidding, but still somehow grooming me to be an obedient and responsible soldier. Or at least a loyal pet, shopping mall purse holder. "Stop crying! I will feed you!" one yelled, as she stuck a bottle in my mouth. If she could only understand me, or would she even care the real reason for my tears? Is this what I have to look forward to? A pre-programmed robot childhood? And if I chose, would I be allowed to leave as the men have, because of these women?

Only two years of age now and I can understand more than they imagine. The constant hand taps which blame the things I do on the terrible twos, and the words, 'You're just like your daddy', follows each tap. So am I being punished for his mistakes, or filled with fear of who I will become? Oh Lord, can I be saved from a life that has just begun?

I must strategize, play the role of a good boy that my father couldn't stand. I will escape this. I must recruit, and I believe I will start here. Yes, daycare - a place we are cared for by the enemy, but if done carefully, we can build something great. I move in stealth, for they have little spies everywhere, little versions of themselves trying to trick us with their delicious snacks, juice, cookies, lollipops and crackers. Even though I stand strong, a few good men have fallen, but I know that for the existence of a true man with a mind of his own, I must stay steadfast and be strong for the others that stand by my side. For those that still have their so-called male role models in their lives, I must paint the picture of a future to come. I must make them understand that the ones they call men, could become now-and-then faces, or eventually a memory of an insubordinate who tried to think on his own and was perhaps replaced with another face. I can't lie, but sometimes I am confused by the trickery and deception that I feel is constant.

When I lay there cold at night, she embraces me with her warmth. I remember me talking to my unborn sibling, as I lay upon her belly, subliminally instilling what he must know to survive, mixed with a few words of my eagerness for him to arrive. My eyelids were lowering towards a deep sleep, only to be lifted quickly from the sounds of pain. Standing bent over me in a pool of liquid, was my mother.   The older one, who she referred to as mom, called for back-up. I wasn't too sure, but I hoped that this was the moment, which I'd been waiting for. The arrival of another person who shared my DNA and gender.

As I follow behind those that came in, with all kinds of instruments and their loud car with rotating lights, I am held back by the old lady who was ensuring the well being of my brother. 'Who knows what they will do?' my mind shouted. 'Once they have him, he may not return!' It's then when I start to believe that the women are probably taking him to alter his perception of what's really going on. I begin to weep, but not for a bottle or changing of my diaper, but for not knowing what was going to happen.

"Positive thoughts", I chanted. "Come on, man. Don't think negative." Days go by, and the honking of a horn outside the house and the smile from the old lady showing many teeth where sometimes there is none, picks me up. I head to the door and there she is. My mom. After days of torture, she approaches us with the little bundle, and then kneels on the floor next to me. "No!" I screamed. "It can't be! Where is he?"

She has brought another girl into the house, and I do believe now the conspiracy of it all. I do believe now that we are to be annihilated to the point of extinction. My brother must have resisted. He heard the talks I had given him while he sat in the womb, and like a true warrior, for the cause he fought, they turned him into a girl. You see, that's what they do, but I must be diligent. I must play along so that they won't suspect, and I will use their new powers to get what I need. Another girl! *ugh* I will show her.

Weeks go by and my patience is thin. Every time I try to get next to her, mini me, my mother remains stuck by her side as though they are Siamese twins. So much more attention was being given to her than me, but I will have my chance. Wait a minute! Isn't that my rattle? Although I don't use it anymore, it's for my amusement. It belongs to me and I'm getting it back! "Mine!" I say loudly, as I reach for my toy.

She cries, but I don't care, and like a damsel in distress, mom comes running to her rescue. Once again, taps were given to my bottom, only these are lasting longer than I remember. Once again, the taps were followed by, "You're just like your daddy!"

I suddenly realized that I'm glad that I'm not, because the negative comparison never turns out well. Instead, I won't be him, I will be a better me. I will show them, they'll see.

SOUL KITCHEN

By

Marcus Blake

The muffled sounds of the television were blaring beneath the sound of the piano as I composed a jazzy little piece that had been in my head for a few days. I didn't know what the song was, but as a musician and masquerading artist I was compelled to work out the symphony in my head.

What I didn't know was that the song inside of me would awaken the part of my youth where I truly learned what music was and that it would become an anthem for my sorrow and joy for one of America's greatest places.

The reports that were coming over the television were ones of a great disaster that had taken place in the city of New Orleans. Hurricane Katrina had hit the city hard and furious, sending the city below sea level and its inhabitants fleeing with only a few belongings and the clothes on their backs.

I could hear the reports on the television, but couldn't believe it; I had to see the television with my own eyes. There were pictures on the news of this beautiful city destroyed by nature's own hand and all I could think was that a special part of who I was, a part of my youth was being taken away with it.

I had spent some time in New Orleans when I was a young man and this was the place where I truly learned music and the very nature of how it lives inside of us. It was one of the best times of my life and also where the world was truly opened up to me.

My name is Jason and I teach jazz composition at a small community college in the Chicago area and still do some studio work and orchestration for jazz musicians when they come through Chicago. Music is my life, it is my passion, but I would never have known how it could live inside of me without being taught by musicians in the Soul Kitchen of America.

After hearing these reports of the city of New Orleans being destroyed by a hurricane I was feeling the disbelief that it couldn't be true. Then the deepest of sorrows found me and I knew for the first time that it was true. The rest of the day I stayed glued to the television trying to find out all I could about what was happening.

A few hours passed by since hearing the first reports and my wife finally returned home. She looked at me with great concern because I could not take my eyes off the television and she even tried talking to me, but I couldn't hear her because my attention was completely on the television screen.

I was deep in memory, I had returned to a place within my youth; the happiness I had felt when I was in New Orleans. I was remembering the time that I had spent there trying to be a professional musician and when life was truly open before my eyes. I finally responded to my wife's questions,

"Honey, I'm sorry," I began. "I didn't mean to ignore you, it's just that I can't take my eyes off the news. They're reporting that a major hurricane is hitting New Orleans and the city is being destroyed by water."

"It's okay, I was wondering what you were watching so intently," she said, "I heard about New Orleans on the radio. It looks like it's going to be a bad one."

"It's going to be worse than that," I said.

"Well, I know that the city will be destroyed, but they can rebuild it," she said.

"That's not what I was talking about," I said.

"What do you mean that it'll be worse?"

"A part of our culture is being washed away with this hurricane, and a part of my youth   that was very special to me is disappearing."

"I'm sorry. I didn't know New Orleans meant that much to you," she replied.

I didn't know how to explain it to her. I didn't know how tell her how much this city meant to me. We had been married for a few years now and she had told me all about the time she had spent in Paris. We had spent countless hours talking about how much being in Paris had changed her life like something out of a Hemmingway Novel or Audrey Hepburn movie, but I had never told her about the time I had spent in New Orleans.

I knew my wife very well by the stories she would tell of how Paris changed her as a person, but I had never allowed her to really know me and how music became so much a part of my life because I had lived in New Orleans for a while. As I watched my favorite city and the place that brought me into adulthood being destroyed on the television I found the courage to finally tell her about this point in my life.

"I've never told you about the better part of a year that I spent in New Orleans and how I finally grew up while being there?" I asked her already knowing the answer.

"You've never said anything about that to me," she said. "How did New Orleans change you?

"In the same way Paris changed your life," I said, "New Orleans changed mine. It's where I truly learned what music was."

"I thought you learned to play the piano as a child and by studying it in college. Isn't that where you also learned how to be a professional musician?"

"Sure, that's all true, but through all that I didn't truly learn music," I said. "I learned the true art of music in New Orleans over the eight months I spent there trying to be a professional musician."

"Well, I think it's time I finally hear this story, don't you think?" she asked.

I just smiled at her, got up to get us a drink and replied, "It may take a while, but yes, it's time. You know how sometimes you'll say you don't know me at all when it comes to me playing the piano because I enter a different world?" With a surprised look she responded with a nod and then I told her, "After this story you will, and you'll finally have a part of my soul."

My wife and I didn't talk a lot because I didn't have a lot to say to her. It was easier for me say what I felt in music. This story was hard for me to tell because for so long it was the one part of me that nobody had a piece of and I always knew that the people close to me couldn't understand it.

I didn't know for sure if I could trust my wife to understand and not hold it against me, but I also knew that if we were going to have a future and a strong relationship, then I had to give more of myself to her. So I finally began my story of why New Orleans was so special to me.

When I was about 19 or 20 years old I took my first trip to New Orleans. I was going to college in Texas on a football scholarship and bartending on the weekends at some little college joint called Dixie's. It was spring break and some of the girls I worked with at this bar thought it would be fun to go to New Orleans for a couple of days.

One of the girls I worked with was from there and wanted to show those of us that had never been one of the "best places on this damn earth", as she called it. So there I was on my way with two girls I hardly knew driving down to New Orleans, about to enter a world that I had only read about in books, but not very nice books.

When we got there we found one of the last rooms available and it was in the most luxurious hotels in New Orleans, the Omni Royal Orleans hotel. Somehow we got a good price and I assume it had something to do with the girl from New Orleans knowing somebody there, but that's how one usually gets things in a city like this. It was a beautiful hotel right in the heart of the French Quarter; we were only a ten minute ride on the trolley from where the action was on Bourbon Street. Now when you're young there's only one thing you want to do in New Orleans and that's party. That we did, for about two days straight in a town that really never sleeps, where the music is always playing from the dingy jazz halls to the street corner musicians.

The partying was fun and even making love to two beautiful women in a big comfortable bed while being serenaded by jazz musician on the street corner down below was nice, but it wasn't the thing that made me fall in love with this city.

The music I heard in every joint we visited and the songs from every street corner musician I passed were like heaven's sound mixed with exotic lust where you couldn't help but give into temptation without the worry of your falling soul. I don't think the girls I went with were that keen on the music we heard compared to the liquor we had every night, but as for me, my soul was lost to the music and I knew I would never return.

We only stayed for two days and I only got to see the French Quarter while we were there, but that's all it took for me to be hooked. I knew I had to be a part of it, a part of this "no need for words" music scene, especially after the first night we were there and I got to jam on the piano with some jazz musicians in one of the joints we had visited. Now this feeling I had could have been from the standing ovation I got for my playing and the owner offering me another chance to play, but when I was on stage I felt that I had just been born and that was what it was like to be alive.

I went back to the Texas town I was living in at the time, but not after leaving part of my soul to be stored as a keepsake in the Soul Kitchen of America.

Home and college for me wasn't the same after this trip because I felt like a part of me was missing and I knew I had to find it. However, unlike many who lose a part of themselves and then spend a lifetime trying to find it, I knew where I had left myself. I wasn't back too long, maybe a few days, before I felt like I had to go back to New Orleans.

At the time I had nothing holding me back, not even my college education. There was nothing to keep me in Texas, so I packed some of my things, moved out of the house I was living in with some roommates, and drove south to a place called The Big Easy.

I didn't have a plan. I had no sense of what it truly meant to struggle as a musician and I had no idea of the true nature of New Orleans. I didn't know how this city could claim a man's soul while at the same time destroying him from the inside out and then remaking him into a true human being with passion and soul; the two things that give us the means to really, really live.

When I arrived I stopped to breathe the air, to breath in the beginning a new life, and a chance for a remodel in who I was. I was here to try my hand at being a professional musician.

The first place I stopped at was the little joint where I first played music in New Orleans, The Blue Nile Club. It was a little dingy place with old dirty wooden floors that creaked a soft melody of experienced jazz and was filled with the smell of smoke and cheap bourbon. It was the best place for true music, the music made from true human experience and sorrow, the music of life.

It wasn't the most glamorous of joints, but it was real and it was the best place to learn the very nature of music. The stage was in the furthest corner of the place, but it was the very underbelly and soul of The Blue Nile Club.

I walked in, and as I tried to take in all that the place had to offer, the bartender came over to me and said in kind of an annoyed tone,

"Are you lost, can I help you find your way?"

"Perhaps you can," I said. "I played piano here about a week ago in some open mike night with a bunch of local jazz musicians and I was looking for the owner of the place to see if I could get some other gigs."

"Well we get a lot of piano players here; you'll have to be more specific," he said, obviously still annoyed.

"I played with some guys that hang out here a lot, I think one of them is called Sam and I got a standing ovation the night I played."

"That doesn't really help me, but if you played with Sam then you might actually be good. Let me get Dave, the owner."

The bartender went to the back to get the owner and the both of them walked out together. Dave seemed to recognize me as he walked toward me, but it was apparent he didn't remember my name. He shook my hand and said,

"Well it's the piano kid who got a standing ovation about a week ago. I was wondering if you were ever going to show back up at my place again."

"I'm here and I'm looking for work as a piano player," I said.

"I don't have anything for just a piano player; we mainly get jazz bands to play at The Blue Nile."

"Oh, well I need to find some kind of work as a musician, I just moved down here to see if I could make as a professional musician."

"Hold on there, kid, it takes time to get to that level and you have to pay your dues. I already know you haven't done any of that yet or I would have heard of you long before last week."

"I'm willing to start somewhere. Hell, even you said I was good enough to do this business after playing that night and the standing ovation I got."

"You're good, I'll give you that, but I don't know if you should've moved down here and given up on college to try and pursue this. If you're willing to start somewhere then maybe we can accommodate you in some way."

"Thanks, I'll start anywhere I have to."

"Well I hear Sam needs a piano player in his little jazz band since his other one died from old age. If he'll take you on then you can start playing with his band here about three or four nights a week."

"Hey, I'll take anything I can get."

"Good, because it's about the only thing you're going to get as a musician around here. Musicians are like bums and drunks in New Orleans: they're everywhere you turn. "

About an hour later Dave had located Sam and his band to see if they might be interested in me. I was nervous; the only thing I'd had to eat was some complimentary gumbo at The Blue Nile to which I couldn't begin to describe the contents of. It was tasty, but like most Cajun food it was good because I didn't know what was in it.

Sam gave me an informal audition and after about three songs and jamming with his band I had the job. However, just because I had a job didn't mean I was good enough to be there, but this is where my true education would begin.

Sam was an old jazz musician who had been playing in cathouses throughout New Orleans since he was about ten years old, and he still had the lungs of a young boy to blow a trumpet. He was well traveled and had been a part of many jazz ensembles from the west coast to the east coast, even jamming once or twice with Miles Davis.

He never knew for sure if he had played with him one or two nights because he was too drunk to remember, but not drunk enough to play music from his very soul with one of the greats. He had settled back in New Orleans after spending about 25 years on the road and decided to dedicate himself to producing young jazz talent that could have the stuff to make it. He had formed and broke up about a dozen bands since he settled back here, always looking for the perfect mix of music and soul in a group of musicians to play what he called "the real thing".

Now he had five other members of his band. There was Jonesy, a cross eyed drummer with glasses thicker than a microscope, but he never missed a beat. He was the quiet one who only expressed himself with the soft beat of the drums.

There was Rick the bass player who never quite felt comfortable with an electric bass and had hands that stretched the entire handle reaching down to find the deep notes of the song and the soul. There was Marc the trombone player, who was never seen without a smile on his face or a joke to tell anybody who would listen. He had one hell of a sweet melody when it came to jazz. Then there was Jerone the saxophone player whose talent could rival Coltrane himself.

It's bold to say such things, but it's true, and he was also the smart ass of the group. As much of a jackass as he could be, you couldn't help but like him, but there was always one problem that consumed him. He was a heroin addict, and it was just as much a part of him as jazz. All of these guys were street musicians who had been playing all their lives. They were thrown together as one of Sam's last creations, with a sweet melody that could reach deep inside someone and find the purest form of love. As good as all of them were, Jerone was probably the one musician who could make it and become a legend.

This was the group I was thrown in with and would learn from; I would learn much more than music, I would learn many different shades of life that I had only heard about as if it were legend. So there I was, a part of this little jazz band within a day of moving down to New Orleans, and the next night I had my first gig with them at The Blue Nile. I can't say I was that good, but I had a place to learn and some of the best musicians to learn from.

Being part of a jazz band isn't like jamming with some local musicians in a garage somewhere, where the only thing you do is just play music. When you're in a jazz band there's more than just playing the music, there's finding the perfect balance of rhythm and harmony, the basics of living life.

You have to be in sync with every member of the group to create the perfect harmony, the perfect wave of tempo. Jazz is about feeling, it's about living the songs that are being played because they are part of your very soul. This is what I was taught when it came to jazz and the road to this understanding was just part of the education I would receive while in New Orleans. This was the real education I got from Sam.

I can't remember if the jazz band I played with had a name or not; for the most part we were just referred to as Sam's Jazz Band because everybody knew Sam throughout the clubs in the French Quarter. We would play about three nights a week at The Blue Nile and there were also other places that would give us a gig.

All in all, we played five or six nights a week and sometimes in the afternoons on the streets throughout the French Quarter, depending on what kinds of events were on the calendar for the tourists. There was music on every street corner and music in the parks was a big thing for the city. As professional musicians we played anywhere we could, and anywhere we were offered money.

After every gig there was usually time for drinking and other things, which was a pastime for professional musicians. I had never known this, so after the gig we played I would be inducted by ritual to the musicians great past time of unwinding. I wasn't old enough to drink legally, but that didn't matter in the French Quarter; if you could see the bar then you were old enough to drink. I wasn't too big of a drinker either, but I would be initiated by good southern whiskey. Sitting around, drinking, and just hanging with one another could last for hours even past closing time.

Everybody in The Blue Nile was like family so I don't remember ever really paying for a drink; we would just sit around as if we had known each other all our lives and this could go on till dawn. I have never felt more at home in an unfamiliar place than I did at The Blue Nile.

As all the other guys would sit with their drinks and jawjack with one another while flirting with the women parading through the club, some local and some doing the tourist thing, I would mainly sit around and just listen. I really didn't know that much at that time in my life so the best thing for me was to sit and listen.

I hadn't really lived life up to that point and college is just a small part of life. You have to get out there into the world to see every aspect of it to really know what life is, to really be educated in things. Sam knew that this wasn't me and that's why he always referred to me as the rookie. So after my first gig with the band he got me a girl, which really is like a rite of passage for passing into manhood in a strange sort of way.

"Until you've done it with a working girl," Sam told me, "you don't know what the sweet lowdown really is." That's where you find that things can be sweeter in the bottomed out hollows of life because they're more real and they never hide behind masks. Sleeping with a prostitute and not having to pay, especially one that can teach you a few things, is just one of those things.

You might not believe me, but the best education a man can receive in life is being taught how to be a great lover, because we are never born with some great erotic instinct. Talent in the bedroom has to be taught and the best time for this is when a man is young so he can be taught by an older woman who has been around and will never fail to tell you the truth. Unfortunately young girls still have the problem of extreme exaggeration, and yes this is just one more thing that Sam would teach me about life.

The girl Sam found for me and the one that would teach me talent in the bedroom was a local working girl named Melanie. She was regular at some of the less classier strip joints who offered more than just dancing topless. She was in her thirties, although no one knew her real age and was one of the most beautiful women I had ever seen. She was the type of woman that had experienced almost anything imaginable; there wasn't anything that really shocked her. To look at her you wouldn't think she was very smart, but she was very keen about life and there was an artistic side to her that was never seen behind her great physical assets.

She just used what she had to make money, which was more than art can do for you sometimes, although as she would say, sex was just a different kind of art. Looking back, I think it was her artistic side and her dry sarcastic sense of humor that made her beautiful. That's what I loved about her more than anything.

Melanie was the perfect example of someone who hid behind a mask, and you had to go behind it to find out who they really were. She wasn't just a working girl using sex to make money; she was a beautiful artistic soul full of life. Like most working girls in New Orleans, there was more to her than her physical assets, and she was just as full of shit as anyone else; she was normal.

She helped me pass into manhood that night. I wasn't a virgin, but young and immature girls never open your eyes to the truth of the world that's hidden behind the mask of youth. Melanie removed my mask that night and I began to see the word anew; someone who sees it more cynical and with realistic eyes. It was the night of my first gig in New Orleans that the world turned for me, and I was reborn, never to be the same again. I put the childish things away and grew up overnight.

I don't remember a lot of the nights I spent in New Orleans, but no matter how much whiskey I'd had that night, I could never forget the events of my first night there.

All total I would spend about eight months in New Orleans before finally coming home. My nights were spent the same way; music, drinks and lively conversation about the real human philosophy, the experience of truly being alive.

I would stay up almost all night, every night hanging out with the band and the half dead inhabitants that would come and see us play. While this went on I was getting to know a different class of people. They were people I had only read about from books of the Beat writers or a Faulkner novel, real people trying to find something to sustain them in their sheepish lives, like soulful music or smooth whiskey.

During the days I saw New Orleans and the heart of the city. I visited the usual places like the cemeteries, the Garden District with houses that were built in the Civil War era, all of the French Quarter, and even the Voodoo Museum. I saw every historical site there was in New Orleans, but the real substance of the city came from visiting the places that aren't found on maps.

They're the places that we don't want to know exist because they're the ugly side of life. It's that place where pimps, prostitutes, gamblers, junkies, and people who have nothing left to lose hang out; there in the back alleys and dark buildings where most tourists never stray. I even ventured to those kinds of places just to see with my own eyes what they were really about and hopefully come out with a better understanding of life's darker side.

I saw more than I probably should have, and whatever innocence I had left after those moments vanished with a whisper. One day on my exploration into those places I saw Jerone there getting his fix to feed the monkey that had been on his back for so long. He had a desperate look on his face as he dealt over the money to his dealer. It was as if he was trying to say without words that it was this which was the only thing keeping him alive, and he would do anything to have it.

I had only been there about two months when I saw this, and Jerone never knew that I had seen him that day. Up to that point, I hadn't realized how much of a problem he really had, but you would never know it by the way he played. The heroin never affected his genius on the sax and it was the only thing that it didn't affect.

I tried to get to know Jerone while I was playing in the band, but he never let me, and I think it's because he never liked me. Maybe it was because I was white and just a young cocky kid posing as a musician. However, it seemed he was always in a bad mood and was mad at the world. There were moments when he was pleasant to be around, and after sharing those rare moments with him I like to think it was the drugs that affected his mood. Everybody in the band would cling to that notion.

I tried to get to know everybody in the band while I was there, but most of them were hard to know. The only two people I really did get to know were Sam and Marc. Sam would talk to me a lot because he had a lot of knowledge to pass on to me.

He knew right off that his role in my life would be as a teacher, so we would spend a lot of time talking about music and spending time on the road. Marc, on the other hand, as seasoned as he was in playing jazz just simply loved people and loved talking to people. It was hard to shut him up, but as I look back he was an absolute delight to talk to because he was always talking about something funny. I don't remember not ever laughing when I was around him. Looking back, I don't feel like I really knew any of them at all, but maybe I knew enough, and that's all that really matters.

I got to know these men as jazz players, as artists, and as fellow musicians. This is how it is with musicians; we never know the people we play with as the people they really are. We know them by their sound and the music they play, and that's enough.

I don't remember most of the time I spent in New Orleans because most of it is just a blur of smoke and whiskey; my time there was just like a dream. I do remember seeing the city and many of the most interesting parts of it, even the dark underbelly of it. I can remember the smell and look of every club we played in even if I couldn't remember every night that we played.

Each place had its own distinctive look, but they all smelled of smoke and cheap bourbon. It's a smell that has never left me and one that I still love today. I wonder if every jazz or blues joint smells that way; it would be nice because it's the smell of something real. Out of all the things I could remember and couldn't remember there are two moments that stand out in my memory more than anything and they are the two that changed my life the most. The first one would be the one that would make me leave and finally come home.

After being there for about eight months, the band that I played with came to an end. We were getting pretty well known throughout the clubs and getting some good recognition outside New Orleans on the jazz circuit. I guess it doesn't hurt when you get to jam with Wynton Marsalis for a night.

He had come home for a few days and like any musician, you're never home unless you're in a club. We happened to be one of the acts at Tipitina's on a beautiful cool fall night and there he was in the club like a god among mortals. Since we were playing at the time and he liked the sound and wanted to know if he could jam with us for a while, but as I later found out he and Sam knew each other.

They had crossed paths on more than one occasion and they were friends on the only level that musicians can be. They had complete respect for one another and the craft they have. After having a brief conversation with him I can honestly say that I have never met anybody more humbling, nicer, and worthy to be envied.

As our band gained more and more fame and the disbelief started to be stripped away that a white boy could play true jazz on the piano, we became more and more destructive. Our sound was still there and Jerone was still just as much of a master on the saxophone as he ever was despite having more and more problems with the monkey that constantly stayed on his back.

However, that was the thing, his heroin problem was becoming more and more of a problem and he was taking Rick down the same demented path he was on. No matter how high or comatose he became, he could still play and he never missed a note. Even then one could still get lost in his music, his soulful notes, and his true art.

The band members would fight constantly with each at the end of our eight month stay with one another. Jerone would bicker amongst everybody and the only attitude he had toward Sam was one of contempt, just like a teenage child has towards a parent.

Sam would spend more time babysitting everybody towards the end instead of composing and helping fine tune our sound so hopefully one day we could play for more than just New Orleans audiences, but it would never happen. I tried to stay out of most fights because I was still for the most part an outsider, but there were a lot of times that I wasn't at least a little bit drunk so I even had to get in the middle of it sometimes, which just made everybody hate me more except for Marc and Sam.

Sam would constantly say that he was too old for any of this and he was going break up the band because everybody kept acting like children. He never did it because of the sound we had. By the end of our run we had a perfect sound and we were in perfect sync with one another. When that happens everything else takes a back seat because it's very rare when something like that happens.

However, it would never last, because like most great things they eventually pass away into a cold unforgiving night. Sometime in the fall we were back at The Blue Nile after being on the music circuit in New Orleans for a few months. We toured just about every place you could think of where music was allowed to be played in New Orleans and then we finally came home to where I started.

On the night we played I noticed Jerone being even more agitating than usual to everyone in the band. He didn't look well at all, even more so than usual. Rick didn't look good either, and as we started into our set I knew that the both of them had taken a really big hit of the juice, but it never affected our sound that night. We were still good that night and they were still masters of their sound.

After our set was done and we started to clear the stage Jerone, rushed back stage just in time before he collapsed. He hit the floor hard and shook violently. He was overdosing and this time there was no going back or coming out of it.

I was the first one to reach him so I propped him up off the dusty floor trying to get him to stop shaking, but nothing I did helped him. The other members of the band rushed back stage to help, as well as Dave the owner, but nobody knew what to do except Sam. He just told us to hold him still and wait for an ambulance. He had seen this before.

Years of being on the road playing with drug addicts had taught him that the only thing that could be done was to wait for a medic. A shot of adrenalin was the only thing that could save him if the medics could get there in time, but this was the Big Easy and time wasn't something of importance.

All of us just watched in horror as Jerone shook violently while he overdosed, slowly drifting away into restful sleep. He died just as the medics arrived at the club, and all that time I held him slightly off the ground. Jerone died right there in my arms even though he would be pronounced dead a few minutes later after the medics tried vainly to revive him.

They had to try because it was their job, but we all knew he was dead before the medics could try anything. None of us cried except Rick; we just stood there and stared in disbelief, even though we all knew that one day the juice would get the better of him. Today was that day and I can't say for sure if Rick cried out of sorrow or out of some misplaced guilt because he let his friend take too much of a hit that would eventually kill him.

All I know is that he ran out of the club that night as the medics loaded Jerone's body into the ambulance and we never saw him again. Rumor has it that he suffered the same fate in some dark back alley of the French Quarter, but those are just rumors.

Although, fate sometimes has a very sick and ironic sense of humor. And now as I remember back to the two of them arguing with one another before our set I like to think that they argued over the amount of heroin they took and Rick couldn't live with the guilt of his friend dying after taking too much.

I had never seen anybody die before, much less have someone die in my arms, but this event has never left me. Watching Jerone, a true artist and gifted musician, overdose on heroin and die made me look at life in a different way. I have never been careless with my life since then, and I knew that if I was ever going to make it as a musician, I couldn't carry anything with me as to be completely free to flow in the music.

None of us in the band went to the burial service, which just consisted of two grave diggers putting his body in a hollow grave that nobody would ever know the location of. He didn't have any family except fellow musicians and as a musician you can never remember someone being buried; you remember them on a stage playing their music, living their art. That's how I remember Jerone, because that was the only way that I knew him and I can never forget his sound.

As for the band, we never played again, and except for Sam and Marc I never saw anybody else from the band again after that night. To tell you the truth, I never heard about them again either.

The next day I saw Sam at The Blue Nile. He was reading a newspaper at the end of the bar while Marc was cleaning his instrument on stage. They were like two people waiting for a musician to walk in and the show to begin, but that day would be reserved for goodbyes. I knew the band was over and I also knew that I couldn't keep going on like nothing happened.

It had affected me too much and it would be awhile before I would get over it. I had truly grown up in New Orleans, but I still wanted to hold on to some of my innocence in youth and that couldn't happen in the Big Easy.

Sam just looked at me and smiled when I walked over. He knew I was looking for some clarity over what had happened the night before so he offered me a simple philosophy of life wrapped in a few kind words.

He said to me "Pull up a seat my young friend and I'll give you something you need to know."

"What makes you think I need to know anything about last night?"

"Because the lack of understanding is written all over your face, and being as you are, I know that you need to hear some encouragement so you can get on with the rest of your life."

"I've been trying to make sense of what happened, but I just don't get how things can change so fast from one day to the next. I mean, we were going along great then this happened."

"Welcome to the life of a musician," said Sam. "Life is like the notes we play. It's up and down; you never where they can take you. You've never seen someone die before have you?"

"No," I said, "it was the first time I'd ever seen something like that. I've never done any drugs before or seen somebody do them. If that's what it's like seeing somebody die from an overdose then I don't want see it again."

"It understandable, but you've woken up to what the world is really like and how such a gifted artist can be struck down by their own misdeeds. Now you know what true tragedy really is."

"Does it get any easier after something like this?" I asked.

"No, I wish I could tell you it does, but life is full of disappointments and misery. All we do is learn to cope with it and then try to find something not quite so bad that we can call happiness."

The bartender brought us a couple of drinks and some lunch. Sam and I just sat there for a moment sipping on our bourbon while Marc smiled and hummed a sweet Charlie Parker tune in the middle of cleaning his instrument on stage. After a long pause and the burning sensation of the drink had numbed my throat I asked Sam,

"So what now, what do I do?"

"I can't tell you that, you have to figure that on your own, but that's the joy of youth. It's getting to figure it out on your own and make all sorts of mistakes while clinging to the notion that you actually know something."

"Are you going to continue with the band and add new members?" I asked.

"Probably not, but I'll never quit playing. There will always be a song for me to play and a stage somewhere for me to stand on. I just gotta find where that is in due time."

"I guess I could always go on the road and try and make it."

"If you do you won't find anything easier than any of this. Its tough out there and you can end up just like Jerone or Rick."

"I think I'm smarter than that."

"That's got nothing to do with it, we can all fall and when we do we fall hard. That's what the road is. It may seem glorious and romantic, but it's even more dark and brutal to the human body."

"I guess I could always go back to school."

"And you'll be better at it because you've grown up now, your life has been changed while being down here, and probably for the better."

"You think that's what I should do?"

Sam just smiled and let out a light chuckle; then he sat there for a long moment. I thought at first he wasn't going to answer me and he probably didn't want to. However, like a teacher to an eager student you can't help but pass on some kind of knowledge or advice.

Finally he spoke up and said "Alright. You want advice then I'll tell you this: you have to live life like you play your music, with caution, passion, intensity, and vulnerability. True music is about playing how you live and it's with everything you are; that's why you live the music. If you do that the song will never leave you and there will always be a stage for you to play on. Now I can't tell you where you should go or what to do, but you have to live your music and you have to let the music be in you."

That's all he said to me, that was his only advice. Sam was my friend, but he was my teacher more than anything else and he told me all that I needed to know. I knew I was going to go home and Sam knew it, too. He knew what I later figured out; my life was more than the road.

I had more to offer than life on the road could provide me and Sam, being a true mentor, pointed me in the direction to finding that out with simple and profound words. They were words to live by and they are the words that I've carried with me every day. I shook his hand, and then said goodbye to Marc. He hugged me and made me laugh one more time and that was it with the Big Easy for me.

I left New Orleans that day and came home. I hadn't seen my family in eight months and when I came home they knew as I did that I wasn't the same, but it was in a good way. Before I left, I made one last stop to see Melanie.

She didn't say anything and didn't have to, because I was a changed man and in no small way she had a hand in that. All she did was kiss me and give and me a hug then she turned around and I never saw her again. No matter what though, I have never forgotten her and especially one of the most exciting, sexy, erotic moments I ever experienced, posing nude while she painted me.

That experience was the one thing that made me realize, to truly know someone is to go with them behind the mask they hide under. The last thing I did was make a stop at the Mississippi River and throw my spare change in the river as if I were making a wish or paying the boatman not to take me across just yet.

I never saw anybody that I knew down there ever again, even though I visited a few times since then. When I first moved to Chicago I got a postcard in the mail from New Orleans letting me know that Sam had passed away and there was going to be a service for him. The card came in care of The Blue Nile Club and I could only assume that Dave had tracked down as many musicians as he could that Sam had played with to let them know about the service.

I didn't make it, but I had flowers sent for the gravesite. It wasn't a proper tribute, but I like to think

Sam knew he had a profound impact on me and for somebody like him it was the perfect gift.

"I came home a changed man," I told my wife as she sat there with a sorrowful look on her face. "And as I said before, I don't remember a lot of the time I spent there, but I do remember Jerone's death and Sam's words. They have never left me and they are the two things that really changed me. I still remember them as if they happened yesterday and it's been ten years since all this happened."

My wife finally spoke up after hearing this tale and said "Why didn't you ever tell me any of this? I mean, this is the one of the most profound parts of your life and something that completely changed you."

"I don't know, I guess I thought you wouldn't understand."

"Maybe not all of it, but your sense of finding the right sound makes perfect sense after hearing this story. Were you ever going to tell me about living in New Orleans?"

"I figured someday I would take you down there and show you, but since there really isn't a city anymore I thought I should tell you about the New Orleans I knew."

"I'm glad you did and I would have liked to see what you saw."

"You know, everybody has their one special place that really changes them: Hemmingway had Paris, Armstrong had New York, but I had New Orleans and now it's gone."

"They can always rebuild when this tragedy is over and what you had will never be gone because you have it in memory and you have it in your music."

"I guess you're right, but I feel like a home of mine is gone and I can never get it back."

"You may be surprised, you know they will rebuild because the spirit of the Big Easy as you described can't be taken away. I have a feeling that there are too many people like you who feel the same way about that city."

"What do you think is the best way to remember it, through song?" I asked.

"You could do that, but I think when they start rebuilding in the months to come we should go down there and help. You can show me what you took with you that made New Orleans so special."

Months later when the rebuilding process started, I took my wife to New Orleans and we volunteered through the Red Cross. I wanted to show her what this city really was, what I saw in it, and what I learned from it. It was a place more free than other places, where great music and a darker sense of life collide to bring a perfect balance of humanity; the true beauty of the world.

The Big Easy is the true melting pot of America where whites, creoles, and negroes are stewed in thick, sticky, gumbo like stew found below sea level. But what comes out of all that besides a little bit of tragic circumstances is a natural cuisine of true people. From those true people comes a creative expression that we live by and is inside of us, and that we dub jazz. All of this made me a better person, made me more humane, and the least I could was to help rebuild this Soul Kitchen.

The first day that we arrived and started working with other Red Cross and Habitat for Humanity members I saw one of the most extraordinary things. The best example of survival, the best example of true human passion which is what will make this city survive through this tragedy.

What I saw was a wide smiled trombone player standing on a street corner in the French Quarter talking with the crowd of relief workers and making them laugh. Then he started playing a familiar jazz tune from my youth so he could entertain us just a little bit. He was the epitome of Jazz, he was true music, and he was a living art.

Check out more cartoons like this....
www.leftycartoons.com

POETRY

Painting is silent poetry, and
poetry is painting that speaks.

~ *Plutarch*

Magnolia Desert

Blood the pen
Upon sorrows
Of tears of broken
Promises.

Crime of lies,
The poem dies.

Magnolia desert
Of an unwatered
Heart.

Flood the pen,
Upon tomorrow's
Fears of barren
Promises.

Turned to dust,
In this Magnolia desert.

~ Robin McNamara

Being me

Dark chocolate colored eyes,
That mirrors sunsets when sun rays hit just
right.
Caramel covered skin,
the same my ancestors once wore.
Mamá aways called me ¨Chicana¨
Papá always said ¨Que viva la raza¨
I´ll always be ¨Ni de aqui, ni de alla¨
Latina by roots, American by birth,
But Chicana at heart.
Fluently bilingual, rolling my ¨R¨
But misspelling it all.
¨Build that wall¨?
That shit don't faze me at all.
My dark chocolate colored eyes,
don't mirror sunsets anymore.
But mirror agony that´s hidden in my soul.

-Juliana Rodriguez

A Poem for Her

In the silence of her beauty
I consider it my chivalrous duty
To learn every curve of her face
To know every bit of her grace
To know why she screams at night
And the pain she keeps out of sight
To know why she sings out loud
And she drifts in the clouds
Why she sits around to find life funny
And how she has no real care for money
How I can lose her myself in her smile
And stare at her for quite a while
To hear her sweet lingering voice
To learn why she made that choice
To look through her eyes and see
Exactly what she sees in me.

~ T. Gordon Mayhall

We Are Poets

We have the power
To change, influence, and inspire
We won't retire
Because of our strong poetic desire
It's like a burning flame
Our words flow endlessly
They are hard to tame

You have to be a role model or set a good example
We can't keep living the same way
Inform people about right
Wrong needs to stray

We're here to help
We're here to make you understand
Love is what we need throughout this land

Keep trying
Never give up or quit
Stand up for what you believe in
Don't sit

We won't fall apart or fade away
We will always stand together
We are poets
Now and forever

~ Jason O'Neil Williams

Calm

Approach it calm
All you can do
Take a deep breath
Have faith in you

~ Phil Lester

Job

Job interview
Nervous,
It could all change
Life could become
Ever so strange

~ Phil Lester

Check out more cartoons like this....
www.inkygirl.com

Fall Into Me

Fall into me without remorse;
Let me hold you in blackened wings.
I'll rock you to sleep on a lover's course
As the tainted virgin sings.

Follow me into a darkened room
Where broken angels fall,
And all the lingering shadows loom
Against the padded walls.

Lie in a velvet starless sky
And tell me of your pain
Where nighttime breezes seem to sigh
And weep where they are lain.

On a black satin pillow, whisper my name
But never ask me why.
For after tonight, nothing's the same
And tomorrow, dear lover, is nigh.

~J. L. Stroede

COLD COMES IN

Cold comes in
like a blanket
for the warmth
in the folds
of my memories

dampness comes in
like a touch

darkness comes in
like possibilities

wind calls me
like your smile

rain,
like your eyes

love settles
like water finding
its level

~ Tom Geddie

Soul Mates

My love, you and I are soul mates
Ordained by God before we had any dates
God knew it before we were born
And that we had a lot to learn
He planned for us to experience life
Before we became man and wife
The Master molded our hearts to His
So He'd be included in our first kiss
The lord knew, f our hearts were His
Our minds and bodies would do the rest
That is why, when our bodies meet
It touches us way down deep
We will never have just sex or lust
We're soul mates
So God will always be with us.

~ Penny Reyes

When You Are Pregnant with Words

-   For Sister, Bok-Ju

Once you are pregnant with the burning desire of book publishing
And actually you feel the kicks of the words inside of you
And clearly you see the balloon belly of your passion
You just cannot avoid giving birth to that baby
Outside to the big world
Bigger than your own dreamy womb

You just cannot keep that living organ
In the dark place forever and ever
For you will get an everlasting cycle of morning sickness
Way longer this case until the birth
Nauseated between the urge to let the water break
And the command to hold it inside from the
Fear of having a premature baby
Fear of seeing one without a finger
Fear of being judged by neighbors
Those who have never had a child themselves
Those who measure others with their own shadow scale

While you are wrestling with this dilemma
The fast growing creature follows its own speed
So, why not think about other folks who would come
Greet the baby with all their open eyes and ears
Wowing and crying and smiling
How about following your own heart's beckoning
Towards its course?
For the safety of your body
For the sanity of your soul
For the solidity of your world

~ Young Eui Choi

Creativity

An art which surfaces all the things that are
normally unnoticed,
Anything that soothes the mind and soul,
Brings a sparkle in the eyes,
Sets a smile on the face,
Is creativity,
The biggest creator is nature,
Wherein every spec is unique,
And beautiful in its own way,
Every individual is creative,
Self-discovery results in surfacing hidden talent,
Hesitation hides it,
Overcoming the same results in unimaginable
outcomes,
It's time for us to discover the creativity within,
And show the results to the world...

~ Vandana Bhatnagar

What Happened To Me

I used to be
But, now I'm not:
There no longer is a me

No safe haven harbors me
Dream and joy have vanished
Is this the way it must be

A marionette, that's just not me
Rather than live on strings
I simply prefer not to be

I struggle to be free,
To find the path that leads back
To the me I used to be

I used to be
But, now I'm not:
There no longer is a me

I never even said goodbye
To the me that used to be

~ Veronica Free

Please support these cartoons at www.patreon.com/barry

Check out more cartoons like this….
www.leftycartoons.com

In Clover and Mist She Waits

Her limbs tangle twist and kiss the mist
golden tresses bless the air.
With swirls and twirls in dress of white,
an Irish dancer, ghostly slight.

Begin the rapid notes of flute
and bows to whom she only sees,
her blessed feet in clover spurns
the lover destined she to meet.

Her wait, though long, is met with mist.
The clover wet, the bog a fist.
Yet warm remain her lips her cheek,
for when her lover she to greet

Moonbeams dance on skin so fair
as holy sounds blend in the air,
and prickly skin from cold she waits,
forgetting death, her lovers fate.

On every crescent moon she stays
waiting for her lovers sways,
and arms that she shall never hold
the girl with curling locks of gold.

Until the sun breaks forth the day
ending Irish lovers song
she blends with sky and moves along.
Her fate, this Irish dance till dawn.

~ Heather Bansemer

The Dream

He had a dream
he had a dream
one day
Blacks/Whites
living together
in peace.

He had a dream
he had a dream
cut short
by a bullet
now a memory,
a page of history.

He had a dream
Yes, oh, yes
he did dream
some people
don't understand
how dangerous
it is to dream

He had a dream
one day justice
would reign
we would live as
brothers/sisters.
He believed in his dream.

Dreams are dangerous
when the poor
believe, trust, love,
and are committed to them.

~Trinidad Sanchez Jr.

Shooting Star

From the Cosmos he comes
Though his surround is beautiful
He, is cold and alone
Destiny has prepared a place

Where he shall come to rest
He moves through the emptiness
Not knowing he's following a path
To a ball of destruction

Soon to share the fate of the many
Who once roamed the vast

From here we see him burn across the sky
Lighting up the black canvas
Delighting the eyes

He is pulled down
By the giant blue sphere
Its eerie glow ignites his fear

Then the emptiness begins to fill
He slams down hard upon the air
Which others walk so freely in

Bombarded by the force
only moment till he dies
in a ball of flames

Irony lies, where the death of one,
sparks a special moment
For those who happen to see
the closing scenes
Of the drama of his journey

If he could have only made a wiseman

~ Derwin Emmanuel

Kissing is Everything

Kissing is where it starts
Where true passion arises within our hearts
For if love can make our soul sing
Then the instrument we play is kissing which is everything

Kissing tells no secrets or lies
Just like the glory of the flower beneath the sun that will rise
A kiss is pure and last forever in a day
And is the only thing that while standing still can take your
breath away

What kind of world would we have without the kiss
Ah, but the tragedy of all the love we could miss
For it is only in the soft brush of your lips upon me
That awakens the joy inside for all to see

Let me kiss you again and again
To be reborn and for this love to never end
Let me taste heaven and hear their bells ring
And have you touch my soul with your kiss that is everything

~ Marcus Blake

HAIKU
Themes

February 2019 Theme

"Love"

Wintertime Passion
A special, happy house sings
Because she is there

~ Anonynmous

The nighttime whistles
For the greatest love of all
In this time and Place

~ Anonynmous

Why Valentine's Day
It's a one day reminder
That love still exists

~ Anonynmous

Springtime Awakens
And the cold, bitter winds pass
To find love waiting

~ Anonynmous

One Act Plays

The Masseur

By

David Thomas

Setting:

Along the back of the stage is a bar (wooden bar, stools, mirror on the wall with bottles in front of it, etc.) At stage left is a door leading off stage, a high round table with four stools; the table should always be in high light. At stage right are a bed, end table, and lamp all behind a gauzy screen. There should be a wall between the two sets and in the scenes when the bedroom is used the characters leave and enter using the door at stage left and enter the bedroom from backstage or stage right unseen by the audience. A door marked "restrooms" should be between the two sets. Stage front should be slightly lower than the main stage and occupied by people talking and drinking in low light. If the budget won't allow for real people cut outs will work.

Characters:

Steve is in his late twenties and has an "alternative" look (leather jacket, jeans, etc.).

Dean is in his late twenties and has an "up and coming" look (loose fitting suit).

Ann is in her early twenties wearing dance club attire (sexy, revealing).

The bartender is a woman in her mid-thirties wearing a tuxedo shirt with the top two buttons undone.

The masseur is a large male in his early thirties wearing too tight jeans and a black tee shirt with no sleeves.

Scene: 1

Ann and Dean enter the bar at stage left, arms around each other. They wave at the bartender and Ann goes through the bar and into the restroom. Dean sits at the round table where Steve and the masseur sit talking.

Steve: No, no, no! I did not!

Dean: What are you arguing about?

Steve: We are *not* arguing.

Dean: What are you *not* arguing about?

Steve: Who I was friends with in school.

Dean: Me.

Steve: What?

Dean: Me. You were friends with me.

Steve: *(Exasperated)* I know that.

Dean: Then why would you argue about it?

Steve: I'm not!

Dean: *(to masseur)* Why would he argue such a thing?

pause

He should know who he had as friends.

pause

Me.

Masseur: What?

Dean: Me. He had me as a friend.

pause

I just don't see how you could argue with him. He should

know.

pause

How could you? You weren't there.

pause

Were you?

Masseur: No.

Dean: See then. No need to argue.

Steve: We weren't!

Dean: You are now.

Steve: What? I'm what now?

Dean: Arguing. Now. With me.

silence

Steve: There were more than you.

Dean: *(hurt)* How do you mean?

Steve: You were not my only friend.

Dean: I'm sure I wasn't.

Steve: You weren't.

Dean: So admit that's what started the argument.

Steve: I admit nothing but that I am thirsty.

Masseur: Me too.

*The **masseur** gets up and goes to the bar as **Ann** is walking up to the table. **Dean** and **Steve** wave their arms trying to get the **masseur's** attention to order them drinks.*

Steve: He's deaf.

Dean: You're waving.

Steve: Yes?

Dean: So he's blind not deaf.

Steve: So you agree?

Dean: Of course, but short of getting up you and I are no closer to getting a drink.

Steve: It would seem.

pause

(sarcastically) Oh please, let me.

Dean: *(obliviously)* Oh good, thank you.

Steve: *(resigned)* Of course. The usual?

Dean: Nothing but.

*Steve goes to the bar and **Dean** turns to **Ann**.*

Ann: *(touching **Dean** on the shoulder)* That's the guy.

Dean: *(looking around)* What's that honey?

Ann: *(pointing at the **masseur**)* The masseuse who wants to give me a rub.

Dean: *(distracted)* Masseur.

Ann: *(looking around)* What?

Dean: Masseur.

pause

A masseuse is a woman.

Ann: He's not a woman.

Dean: *(looking around?)* No?

Ann: *(kissing him on the cheek)* No silly.

pause lowering her voice and looking at the **masseur**

No, not at all a woman.

Dean: Just so you know one is not that other.

pause

I have to excuse myself for a minute dear, I need to see what's holding **Steve** up.

Ann: *(distracted)* Sure.

Dean goes to the bar passing the masseur who goes to the table and begins talking to Ann, rubbing his hands up and down her arms. Dean goes back to the table carrying a beer and Steve stays at the bar talking to the bartender.

Dean: Hi.

Masseur: *(slowly removing his hands from Ann's arms)* Hi.

Ann: *(flustered)* I…umm…

pause

Have you met?

Dean: No, not as such. He was just having a silly argument with Steve that had no legs.

Ann: This is…

Dean: *(interrupting)* The Masseuse.

Masseur: *(extending his hand)* Masseur.

Dean: *(shaking the **masseur's** hand)* Oh? Indeed. The masseur.

*The **masseur** walks away with a shake of his head and a touch to **Ann's** shoulder.*

Ann: I'm sorry.

Dean: For?

Ann: I should have introduced you earlier.

Dean: Earlier than what?

Ann: Well…

Dean: Never mind, I'm just distracted again.

Ann: *(quietly)* Again.

Dean: *(kissing **Ann** softly)* Don't worry about it.

Steve returns from the bar.

Steve: I managed to steal our table away from that guy and I still don't know who he is.

Ann: *(speaking at the same time as **Dean**)* He's a friend.

Dean: *(speaking at the same time as **Ann**)* He's no one.

Steve: *(looking between them)* Umm…

pause

Of course.

Dean: It was just some guy.

***Ann** walks away unnoticed by **Dean** and meets up with the **masseur** and they both leave the bar stage left and re-enter stage right behind the screen. As the dialog continues between **Steve** and **Dean** they should be taking off their clothes and embracing, eventually it should look as if they are having sex.*

Dean: Do you think the rain will let up?

Steve: It doesn't seem to want to stop.

Dean: Raining for days.

Steve: And days.

Dean: You think it would let up.

Steve: You would think.

Dean: Yes.

pause

Yes you would.

Steve: *(looking around)* So; where is she?

Dean: Who?

Steve: What do you mean who? Ann.

Dean: *(looking around)* I don't know.

Steve: Her things are here.

Dean: Where?

Steve: There. Right there next to you.

Dean: So they are.

pause

Steve: You should know.

Dean: I should?

Steve: Yes; of course!

Dean: What should I know?

Steve: Where she went.

Dean: Why should I know?

Steve: Didn't you come here with her?

Dean: Well yes, I guess I did.

Steve: And I had rather thought you two had been sleeping together for not some little bit of time.

pause

In fact I was under the impression you lived together.

Dean: Sure, I can see where you might get that idea.

Steve: Is it not true?

Dean: As far as it goes I guess.

Steve: What in the world does that mean?

Dean: I'm not sure.

pause

You know, I'm really not sure what it means.

silence as both drink and occasionally look around the bar

Steve: You really should know where she went.

Dean: So you've said.

Steve: *(emphatically)* You should!

Dean: I'm beginning to think you are right.

Steve: Of course I am!

Dean: You harping on it isn't helping.

Steve: Don't you fell odd?

Dean: Odd how?

Steve: Well…

pause

…foolish.

Dean: Up until now I hadn't thought much about it.

pause

Steve: Are you thinking about it now?

Dean: Hmn?

Steve: Now. Are you thinking?

Dean: Actually, I was.

Steve: Good to hear it.

Dean: No, no, you don't want to hear this.

Steve: Umm…that's not what I said but now that you've brought it up; shoot.

Dean: I'm sorry. What did you say?

Steve: I said I'd love to hear your thoughts on all of this.

Dean: Oh, it's not about *(waving his arms)* all of this.

silence

My mom told me this story once, I don't remember how long ago now…

slight pause

She told me this story about the time the Beatles were on the Ed Sullivan show, what, in '65?

Steve: Sure.

Dean: Anyway, she waited and waited and when it was time for the show my mom plopped herself down in front of the tube on the floor, on her knees with her hands in her lap. She was transfixed by what every other woman in the country was.

slight pause

And I guess my dad was a grump even then because he got mad. Can you believe it?

Steve: Maybe he thought she should support American bands.

Dean: *(ignoring Steve)* Said she was acting like a teenager.

pause

That caused quite a fight, she said…

Steve: I can imagine.

Dean: *(ignoring Steve still and looking around the bar)* Where *did* she go?

Steve: How should I know?

Dean: You're the one who keeps asking, I thought you might have some ideas.

Steve: I'm asking? You live with her for God's sake!

Dean: So no thoughts?

Steve: Plenty of them.

Dean: Great! Let's hear them.

Steve: Nope.

Dean: Why not?

Steve: Because none of them are thoughts you want to hear.

Dean: No?

Steve: No you do not.

Dean: How can you say such a thing?

Steve: Easily and from experience.

pause

Dean: She's gone.

Steve: Possibly.

Dean: I don't see her.

Steve: You never do.

Dean: She could have been kidnapped.

Steve: You don't listen.

Dean: *(looking around)* Kidnapped.

Steve: You *never* listen.

Dean: *(still looking around)* God only knows what happened to her.

Steve: And God only cares.

Dean: Where has she gone?

Steve: You don't listen to her.

Dean: Hmn? *(looking at **Steve**)* What was that?

Steve: You don't listen.

Dean: I am now.

Steve: Now seems to be too late.

Dean: How so?

Steve: Where is Ann?

Dean: *(looking around again)* Just what I would like to know.

Steve: Would you?

Dean: Of course I would!

pause

Would you like a beer?

Steve: There! Right there is my point!

Dean: What? That you would like a beer?

Steve: No. It's just…

pause

…never mind. Sure I'll take a beer.

Dean *goes to the bar and returns with two beers.*

Dean: So; you don't think I pay attention to Ann?

Steve: Not as much as maybe you should is all I'm saying.

pause

Dean: Not only did my father lose my mother by being over bearing and suspicious but…

Steve: *(interrupting)* Oh hey man I didn't mean…

Dean: *(holding up his hand)* Sure you did but it's alright, just let me finish. I have apparently picked up that bad habit from him and have lost more than a few great women over it so I try not to carry on like that anymore.

Steve: Okay I can see that but sometimes don't you think it's possible to go to far the other way?

Dean: How do you mean?

Steve: Forget it Dean, drink up.

Dean: No really, how do you mean?

Steve: Don't you think women want to know that you are worried about them?

pause

Kind of show them you care at least a little bit?

Dean: I suppose.

Steve: I would just hate to see my friend be made a fool of.

Dean: Thank you Steve, but just because I don't have Ann in a headlock doesn't mean I don't care or that I'm blind.

Steve: Alright, I'll get off of it now. I was just concerned.

Dean: Thanks. You're a good friend.

Steve: *(raising his glass)* Here's to friends.

*They toast and as they drink the lights go out in the bedroom set and **Ann** and the **masseur** come back into the bar stage left. The masseur walks deeper into the bar and **Ann** approaches the table.*

Dean: Here she is! *(turning to **Ann**)* Here you are.

Ann: Here I am.

Dean: Where oh where have you gone?

Ann: I went out for some air and I ran into the masseur and we got to talking.

Dean: Ah, well then did he rub you the right way?

Ann: *(alarmed)* What?

Dean: Just a joke sweetie, a small one, but a joke none the less.

Ann: *(relieved)* I get it! Rub me the right way and he's a masseur!

Dean: You were always the clever one dear.

Ann: *(pecking **Dean** on the cheek)* You're sweet.

Dean: Are you ready to go home?

Ann: *(gathering up her things)* I am if you are.

Dean: Great!
*pause turning to **Ann***
By the way, you silly goose; your shirt is buttoned up wrong.
*turning to **Steve** and clapping him on the shoulder*
Well, Steve we're going home now.

Steve: *(hesitantly)* Sure. Take care Dean.

Dean: I do care my man, it just may not look like it sometimes.

*Dean turns and helps **Ann** on with her coat and they leave stage left*

Lights Come Up

For Producers: *If you would like to produce this play, then please contact the writer at…*

David Thomas
214-515-8311
draythomas@gmail.com

Check out more cartoons like this….
www.leftycartoons.com

Articles *and* Editorials

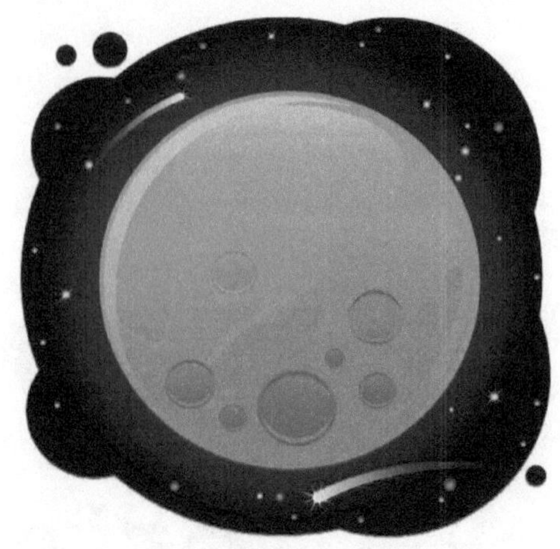

SPACE EXPLORATION

Where Do We Go Next?

By

Joshua Sherman

"We had an expansive run in the '60s and '70s. You might have thought, as I did then, that our species would be on Mars before the century was over. But instead, we've pulled inward. Robots aside, we've backed off from the planets and the stars. I keep asking myself Is it a failure of nerve or a sign of maturity?" Carl Sagan via *Pale Blue Dot*

What happened? So many in the US cheered for the space programs of NASA as we launched so many spacecraft both manned and unmanned into the depths of space towards our nearest satellite the moon. Ever since the return of Apollo 17 we haven't had a manned mission go further than low-earth orbit (leo). I'm more inclined to agree with the late Dr. Sagan that it *is* a failure of nerve on our part, but I think there's even more than that; more like a lacking of public interest. Fortunately a new space race has been under way since the late 1980s, and I'm delighted to say this race isn't predicated on fears of nuclear paranoia.

It's 2017 and NASA's Jet Propulsion Labs (JPL) is no longer the only household name on the block in aerospace. Agencies like SpaceX, Blue Originis, Virgin Galactic, Lockheed, and a handful of other entities are stepping up to the plate to contribute to mankind's quest to usher life beyond Earth into the stars. The question now is where do we set up shop next; and several questions dealing with our basic Pavlovian needs such as shelter, food (and cultivation), and all the necessities for keeping one's environment comfortable enough to live and work and play.

My own suggestion would be to setup a 3-prong campaign that would advance in incremental phases wherein the beginning is a space colony followed by a lunar colony followed by a Martian settlement. The first phase would start with the construction of a politically independent space colony further out than the ISS geocentrically orbits, which is a paltry few hundred miles overhead. A space-born colony makes more sense, as opposed to aiming for another rock, for the sheer immensity of "room" that's available; it's space… plenty of room! The biggest hurdle to overcome is the gravitational difference; not everyone's physiology is suitable to work much less live comfortably in a 0-g environment. Several space station concepts have been introduced through science fiction culture throughout the 20th and 21st centuries that deal with creating the illusion of gravity through a Huygenian principle called centrifugal force (not a real force so much as the consequence of inertial force) including but not limited to habitation wheels, the Stanford Torus, and an O'Neill Cylinder; if you've seen *Mission to Mars*, *Elysium*, or *The Martian* then you have seen the "wheel" or Torus ring in action. These concepts solve the gravity problem, but they also all rely on the one principle; what happens *when* something goes wrong with that system? Let's take Murphy's Law to heart on this. I am not familiar with any pragmatic solutions to the problem of gravitational failure, but if you've ever seen the 2016 film *Passengers* losing gravity isn't anything of a picnic occasion.

So let's put aside the problems of gravity for now. There are still numerous benefits of starting with a space colony and the 0-g environment; think of the drydock that was featured in 2016's *Star Trek Beyond* at Yorktown station. In short, the need to put a space capsule on a rocket and blast it into orbit becomes nullified, and the resources can be put to better use! Another benefit would be that, with all the room available on a large enough space station, mass-production industrial and agricultural endeavors could be undertaken; presently, the ISS has a plant growth system called Veggie that has been running since 2014, and it will soon be joined by a supplemental program called the Advanced Plant Habitat. Imagine a space station that had a dedicated greenhouse for the thousands of species of plant life we have down here!

My own desire would be to take the same agricultural experiment and start cultivating and farming industrial hemp, which has been shown to replace most current mediums for construction and insulation materials; then use the hemp to construct as much of the new space colony as can be accommodated. I mentioned earlier that the colony ought to be politically independent, which would help with cultivation of hemp and many other crops that some nations have prohibited from use or cultivation. There's actually such a space station currently underway that is vying for political sovereignty and recognition from the United Nations, but right now it's only in the logistical stage. *Asgardia*, as it has come to be called, was conceived of by Russian scientist Igor Ashurbeyli. Igor's own desire is to have a colony with no less than 150 million inhabitants from around the world.

Check out more cartoons like this....
www.inkygirl.com

Gaming's Evil Empire

And How to Get back to the Passion of

Creating Great Video Games

By
K. Scott Cooper

Everything on this planet evolves, so do video games. And it's time for some serious evolving in the Video Game Industry these days. Now, before you start rolling your eyes, and thinking "oh gee, it's just another gamer going on and on and on…" Shut up and listen! When I was a kid, video gaming was still in its infancy. I mean, it was a thing; I'm not one of those dinosaurs before it existed, but I've payed my dues. I was poor, so I didn't have the brand-new consoles, and was always behind the proverbial learning curve. That's why when I'm about to name-drop this amazing title, everyone is going to understand where I came from, (well, maybe not all of you, but still). Galaga was my first video game. So this pixilated majesty that I was about to witness when I opened my poor little Irish brain, this wonderful world of disillusion, the moment I popped that game in, hit the power button and heard that "doo-didle-oo!" it was an amazing thing and I was hooked.

For me those early video games had a very loose story, and thus, we were encouraged to make our own. Once we started playing games with in-depth storylines, games changed, and we changed with them. Early gaming it became a contest of who had the biggest, baddest console or platform, as we were seeing the early beginnings of PC gaming as well. At every turn, it was constantly something new, and you were literally traveling through worlds of wonderment, experiencing an enjoyment overload. Honestly, who remembers the first time they popped in "Double Dragon?" Everyone remembers the sensation the first time they got to transform an altered beast, and everyone remembers the first time they got to watch the cinematic scene of Zerg rip apart an ignorant army private for the first time. But we also remember all the pains and credits that came with it too. We remember having to blow into cartridges or jamming a butter knife into the Nintendo so it would stay down, or playing it so long the damn thing nearly overheats and catches fire.

Remember the first time we experienced bug glitches on the Playstation with Legend of Dragoon, knowing half the world wasn't finished yet Us older gamers are in an odd place now. Transitionally, for the much, much older gamer, you remember the time before original gaming consoles, or when they were in their infancy, but we're at this crossroads, where we can remember, but not quite sure if we can like the future of gaming we're seeing. This is because we're seeing the plateau, at the tip of the crescendo, and just like we're seeing in mainstream Hollywood, they just keep redoing the same shit. If I see one more mother fucking Spiderman or Batman game, or one more game that rips off Fortnight, PUBG, League of Legends, World of Warcraft, etc., I'm going to freak the fuck out. We have reached a pivotal point in gaming right now. We've hit the point where it's less about the console and more about the game. Don't get me wrong, it's a fantastic thing, but we need that creative boost that comes from competition. Like striving America vs. Russia cold war arms kind of stuff. And I'm talking, console wars back in the day where you would cut a mother fucker for being a Sega fan, - even though Sega is totally fucking awesome and legit. It's like when they were fighting with each other to be the biggest, baddest console, that was when the hype was real. It was real, and serious, and you could cut that shit with a machete, because it wasn't just in the advertisement or the TV commercials, but how they produced games.

A flop in the market could be the end of a company. But now, there is no fear; no fear of the studio dying, no crashing down, they're simply so solidified now. Because there's no fear, there's no creative spark, nothing to lose means no reason to put forth quality. There is some true creative spark out there, but there's not enough of it, -it's not out there breathing fire like fucking Smaug. And when there is any spark, they're clamoring for it, because it is bang or bust! Since there's so little out there, and because of the over commercialization of the gaming industry, the few creative pools are being too vastly drawn upon, so we're left with repetitious pounding of the meat pile that used to be the dead fucking horse... these people are being over tapped and overdrawn, and due to this, you're left with half finished games. Like we have now.

As gamers we are having serious issues with Fallout 76, No-Man Sky, Mass Effect Andromeda, with them being glitchy as hell and downright shitty games…just to name a few over the last few years. The consumers bitch at the studios for having slow, laggy games, but whereas the studio and software companies are bitching at the consumer, they should be going "ya know what, you're right! But we're limited by the console." And that's the thing. Where the drive ends to be the biggest, baddest console, without that competitive drive there, everything suffers. That's the sure-stead sign that the game has become, in fact, what it has been labeled; an industry. It's no longer a contest, and the fat-cats have all the money. And that's why when you look at the way our games are made now, its all about in-app purchases, VIP exclusive content, and the bigger, badder, triple-platinum-diamond-obsidian, veinier dick like package, so you can get this elusive horseshit that no one fucking cares about at the low, low price of only $128! And it's just… really? What the fuck?…. I still enjoy going back and playing those really old games, like Diablo II, Starcraft, or Battletoads, or all the original Mario games, or speed twinging my wrists in twisting-rage playing sonic the hedgehog.

I still talk about the amazing precedence of that Metal Gear set. It was all anyone talked about. I remember even the goofiest things like Spyro the dragon and Crash Bandicoot, were playable by all, and much to this old player's delectation, to see them alive and revived today. That's what needs to happen. We need to take that dusty ass hat off the shelf, and not take a look at it to see if we can reinvent it, but rather put that shit on our heads. We need to look at the old way of doing video games, bring them back to life, and retell those games' stories, but evolve the system. Instead of using the same old hack the system of whatever is currently socially popular, (Vikings, special agent bullshit, zombies, anything overplayed right now) and throw that shit to the wayside. We need to get the fuck away from that. No more following the trends; we need to be the one setting the trends. We are now at a time where gaming is literally us making the heroic battle of old. Digital bards and poets of antiquity, a I'm happy to see the gaming style of Assassins Creed Odyssey that just came out to dip into that. But we need to not simply dip our toes, but rather to dive in, head first. Take a risk if yuou now what I mean!

So why not take Galaga, make it a space fighter pilot game, inspired by some of the amazing depictions of battles found in the Hindu faith such as the Bhagavad Gita? Where is the new stuff?? We're at a time where we could be telling these amazing, beautifully depicted stories and be actually experiencing them. That is something they touched on ever so gently in the latest God of War. But instead of seeing the North Nantheon and the Greek Pantheon, show me the pantheons of the middle east, of Asia, of the islanders, Give me something new! The Witcher series has done well to introduce us to Slavic folklore, but the problem is, that the shift we're going towards these days is less storytelling, and the build your own adventure you get from multiplayer.

Would it be so much to ask to get an MMO style game where you are inundated with not only the myths and folklore of Mongolia, where you are one of the soldiers rising through the ranks of the great Genghis Kahn. How difficult would it be to do something like that? Well, you might say it's already been done with video games of empire, but is it really? You don't see the numbers, attention, or crowd that you're seeing with Skyrim, because they're just not done well. And because they're not done well, they're not getting interesting, and the vicious spiral spins out of control. The biggest obstacle for them to get the attention and quality deserved is because they're being stifled. What needs to happen is we need to revolve ourselves, and out it into a direction where its useful; most of our games these days look like a stupid little app game bleeding people for money, and it's ridiculous. We don't want to pay $60 to $200 of hard-earned money to be given the same old thing, with the same graphics we've had for the past six or seven years, and the same retelling of the game that came out ten years ago. And we sure the hell, don't want to pay $80 to walk around aimlessly in a game and have no direction.

We need to be rebranding and renaming ourselves. We need the resurgence of healthy competition in games. I'm not sure how best this needs to come along, but it needs to happen. But as it stands right now, we're in a very precarious situation. Do we 100% know what that the future of gaming hold…no. I would love to say that in the past ten years that there has been a game that I just can't get enough of and that I could go back to time and time again. And I'm going to. But the reasons that I like these games are not because they impacted gaming in a big scheme, nor were they such amazing blockbusters that they took everyone's breath away, but rather that they simply spoke to me. Assassin's Creed III was just an amazing take on the American Revolutionary War, and it was this game that brought me into the franchise, which is great, because I'm getting the same experience and the same take on the new Assassin's Creed game, and cannot wait to see where Ubisoft takes us next. But in the way of games like Shadows of the Tomb Raider where they have this amazing female lead and an amazing opportunity to sum up everything about her as the heroine she is supposed to be, then the game ends with very little closure and you're left without any form of satisfaction that Lara Croft is the baddest bitch ever. Instead, you end up feeling like she is a meddling white woman interfering in the lives of the indigenous peoples and is directly the cause of the death of hundreds of thousands of people of color, in my humble opinion. What kind of message does that send?

Game designers and developers have the huge responsibility to tell better stories and to expand on our horizon in gaming, not just be degraded by it. We should be pushing ourselves for the biggest and most bad ass experiences gaming can provide us; we are just getting to the point to be doing things in VR, but we've arrived here too late in the game! We should've already been here in 2009! It's 2019, where are my flying cars, why do we still have load screens, and why don't I have VR so realistic that I can feel the blood spray on my face as I splay an Orc with a serrated blade forged in the Dwarven flames Rexius Omega Prime??? The answer to all these questions and more is simple: It needs to stop being corporate and go back to being about passion.

Baseball Fan 101

By

Emily Stevens

For those of you who are blessed to have a professional baseball franchise nearby, please take advantage of it and go to a game this summer. It will give you a chance to get either out of the heat or soak up the rays depending on which stadium you go to. But before you go to the game please follow these simple rules to make sure that you and everyone around you has an enjoyable time watching the greatest game in the world.

1. Never start or participate in the wave. I don't think any further explanation should be made. If you do start or participate in it, others will mock you relentlessly.

2. If you are going to make a sign make sure that you adhere to the following guidelines.

    A. Make it colorful and neat. If you are going to take the time to bring something into the stadium put some pride into it.

    B. Do not take the easy way out and make some acronym out of the broadcasting channel that is presenting the game (i.e. FOX or ESPN). This shows no real creativity and a sad attempt to guarantee television air time

    C. Make sure that you hold it up the right way, nothing is more embarrassing than seeing some poor soul standing there with their sign displayed upside down.

3. Pay attention to the game. Do not just sit there and socialize about the latest gossip or your latest work assignment. People around you don't really want to hear about it   If you want something to talk about, talk about the game. If you don't understand or know much about baseball a baseball game is pretty good way of getting an education about it.

3. Do not talk on your cell phone. There are plenty of places and times that are available to use it. A baseball game is not one of those times.

4. Not every fly ball hit out of the infield will be a home run, so don't act like it's going to be, it will just make you seem like an idiot.

5. If you are going to buy sunflower seeds or peanuts, make sure you depose of the shells properly. And that does not include over the rail if you are in an upper section, nothing is more disgusting than getting a chewed up sunflower shell on your head.

6. If there are children around you, watch your language. There are few things in this life that are less tactful than a bunch of drunks cursing up a storm with a bunch of families around. Yes, it is a baseball game, but be respectful.

7. If you are going to talk baseball at least have some sort of understanding of what you are talking about because if you are talking loudly enough and if you have a sense of arrogance in your ignorance, others who know better than you will silently mock you.

8. You are not too cool to stand up for the seventh inning stretch. So stand up, enjoy the chance so sing out of key with the rest of the stadium.

10. Enjoy the game. Embrace the drama and never leave in the bottom of the ninth, you really won't beat the traffic and there's a great chance that you may miss out on the most exciting part of the game.

Well, I hope you take these lessons to heart because they will make your experience at the game so much better, I know it will make mine.

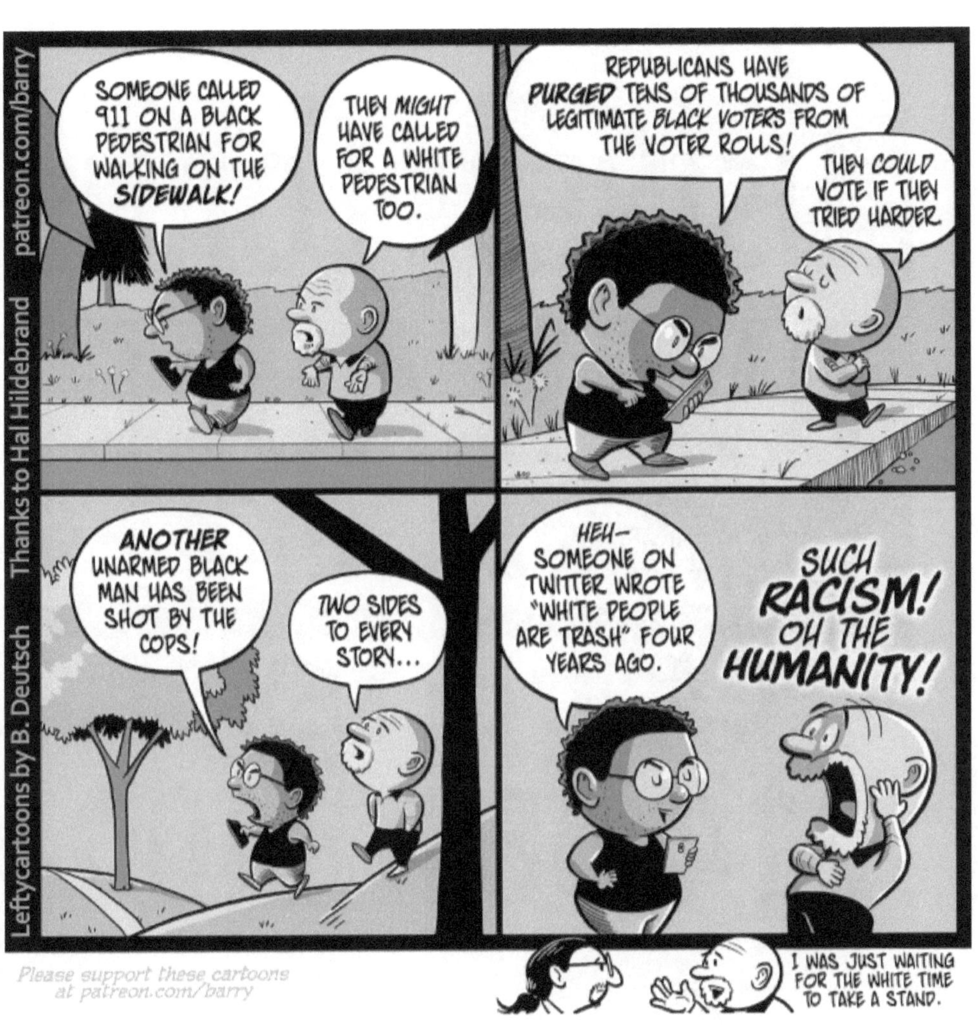

Check out more cartoons like this....
www.leftycartoons.com

BUSINESS LOANS
AVAILABLE
APPROVAL RATE: 94.4%
CALL or TEXT
214-681-8400

A MIXED BAG *Of* FACT and FICTION

Saving Money on Teargas

How the NRA Can Stop Illegal Immigration with Bullets and No Wall

By Bob Jensen

It's another week of a government shutdown in the United States with neither political side budging over the issue of five billion dollars to build a wall on the border of the United State to help keep illegal immigrants from getting into our country. It's the biggest issue we face these days. It's bigger news than what Democratic candidate will be running for president in 2020 or the latest in all of the Donald Trump investigations. Some call it a matter of National Security. Others call it political wrangling over an issue that'll never get solved, much like the United States War on Drugs. But as both political parties argue and debate, call each other names, and see who can be the most petty when it comes to the issue, the one thing that has escaped all sides is fervent solutions. That is until now.

Last week, the President of the United States, Donald Trump declared a National Emergency regarding border security. Instead of using executive orders to raise the money to build a wall, he came up with another solution. It's a solution that dates back to the American Revolution and the years of having civilian militias. He was quoted as saying to a senior White House official, "if we can't build a wall and we will find civilians who want to volunteer to help guard our borders. That will be our wall." In a stunning new initiative, the president invoking a John F. Kennedyesq challenge to the American people, *asking not what their country can do for them, but what they can do for their country* when it comes to border security, has asked for volunteers with guns to guard the border. It was no surprise that this new initiative came with controversy. While some citizens have been very eager for a chance to do this with one man from Texas being quoted as saying "I might finally get to use my gun and shoot someone," some have criticized that this new policy is inhumane.

I was curious to see how all this would work so I traveled to El Paso, Texas along the border to see how this new policy would be implemented. Basically the president is asking for civilian volunteers and you can sign up at any border security office or Homeland Security office, but you have to provide your own gun. The government will not give out guns to any citizen without a proper background check. But government officials freely admit that any citizen can walk into a gun show, purchase a gun without a background check, and sign up that day to be a volunteer border security agent. Conservatives have praised the idea. One man told me that it's a great way for Americans to take responsibility for their country and to give back. What I also found is that while the government is pushing this idea you still need large organizations to help with the Grassroots activism in order to get people behind the idea. And there is no better organization than the National Rifle Association. Last week the president in a sit-down meeting with the president of the

NRA asked how the organization could help when it came to marketing the idea of volunteer border security agents.

One of the ideas that came out of the meeting was to encourage hunters. As with the original intent of the NRA gun club for hunters who advocated gun safety the President of the NRA proposed that why not make another form of hunting season, But this time instead of hunting game they can volunteer for border security and hunt illegal immigrants. After all, he was quoted as saying "they are a threat to American security so why shouldn't they be hunted." During my investigation, I had a chance to sit down with the president of the NRA in order to get some clarifications about his ideas and as I found out, to which the president of the United States agreed with.

The president of the NRA told me that what they would like to do is encourage every able-bodied gun owner who believes in America to help man the border and to use their skills as a hunter to stop illegal immigrants from crossing illegally What I wanted to know is was he was proposing giving every NRA member a license to kill anybody who illegally steps over the Border. He said, "if it is legal to shoot trespassers on your own land in America, then why not illegal immigrants because they are the greatest trespassers of all." I also asked him if that meant shooting women and children. He responded, "of course we wouldn't shoot children because of our current policy of rounding them up and putting them essentially in prison camps." I asked if he thought that this was a little inhumane. What he told me was shocking. He was quoted as saying, "it's more important to protect American interest in to show humanity, especially with enemies you are coming across the border because essentially anybody could come across including terrorists. " I asked if he thought women and children were terrorist and he told me, "just because they don't wear a suicide vest doesn't mean they can't be terrorists.

As you can imagine the controversy with this new policy and the National Rifle Association keeps growing and more than usual. But polls show that the majority of Americans are in favor of a volunteer border security force, although it should be pointed out that most people didn't know exactly what they were going to get to do if they did volunteer. Most of the citizens who volunteered have said, "I'm glad we actually get to shoot someone without going to jail." A lot of democratic and liberal lawmakers have pointed out that that's the best part of America should be showing our humanity to the rest of the world and being able to learn from our own dark history. Especially, that time in American history where we rounded up every Japanese-Americans and put them in internment camps without due process because they might be an enemy of the state. The President of the United States for the most part ignored comments like this, but when he was asked last week in a press conference why the need for this volunteer border security force without any limitation on being able to shoot illegal immigrants, in his usual whimsical manner, simply replied "well if nothing else, it will at least save the taxpayers from having to spend money on tear gas!" Because as one Senior White House Official said, "that's more important than coming up with logical solutions on border security."

Bob Jensen
Reporter & Columnist

The Squeeze
The more true news network!

NUKE
TWEET

500 FREE
Business Cards

Premium Cards, 14pt Card Stock,
Full Color, Front and Back,
Glossy or Matte Finish

Call Today
(888)
901-4665

www.bizproshop.com

Email us to find out how you can get 500 FREE business Cards. info@bizproshop.com or call (888) 901-4665

SUBMIT

We are always looking for submissions. We are looking for Short Stories, Poetry, Editorials and Articles (Non Fiction) and Cartoons / Comic Strips.

Submit your work to www.starvingwriters.net

Email us your submissions at…

submission@starvingwriters.net